Madame Howell's Book of Very Bad Things:

A Baker's Dozen of Frightful Fairy Tales

Volume 1

By

Jae El Foster

DCL Publications, LLC

www.thedarkcastlelords.net

DCL Publications, LLC

First Edition December 2020

DCL Publications
1033 Plymouth Dr.
Grafton, OH 44044

ISBN 978-1-7362178-1-8

This is a work of fiction. Names, characters, places and incidents are the product of the author's imagination, and any resemblance to any actual persons, living or dead, events, or locales, is entirely coincidental.

Cover photo and design by Jae El Foster

Cover Model: Mary Craig

PUBLISHED IN THE UNITED STATES OF AMERICA

"If you want to tell grown-up fairy tales,
you have to look for the dark side."

~ Juan Antonio Bayona

Table of Contents

Dedication

This collection of fanciful perils is dedicated in part to the 'face' of Madame Howell, my friend and soul sister Mary Craig, who is always game to put on the costume and show her witchy side whenever I need. It is also dedicated in part to the 'voice' of Madame Howell, the incomparable Catharine Perkins, whose narration of the Madame is everything I could have ever hoped for. Thank you, ladies, for bringing my character to life in ways that truly entertain!

A Foreword from the Author

Greetings and welcome to this special collection of sinister and otherwise 'fractured' original fairy tales. Our narrator for this collection is a character called Madame Howell, who first appeared in my short novella 'To Adventure' in the anthology *Enchanted Fairy Tales*.

Since then, the Madame has made several guest appearances in my work, including a large role in my fairy tale novel *Beauty Within*. She quickly became a favorite character, and now I'm immensely excited that she has her own collection of wicked fairy tales and lore. While Madame Howell does not appear in any of the thirteen stories you're about to read, she is your guide and companion through them. I hope you enjoy this intimate moment with one of my greatest and most dubious characters.

The following stories are a tribute to the old horrific tales of the Brothers Grimm. One tale, 'Rescued from the Dungeon,' is a toned-down version of a story that was to be released in an anthology of the same name. That original story has been lost to time, but I am pleased to present it to you now in its new, shorter format.

Fairy tales have been around for as long as storytelling and imagination have existed. While there are numerous elements of classical fairy tales captured in this collection, I have presented a lot of new twists that either haven't been tried before or that I have not been privy to. You won't find the slumbering princess or the poisoned apple, or even the wicked stepmother in this collection.

I present to you instead a collection of cold-hearted royalty, demonic creatures, the world's smallest people, and disobedient children who have gone too far… along with so much more. There are magical and inexplicable trees, rats that can speak, secrets to eternal youth, and a house with a rather slithery past.

I hope you enjoy this baker's dozen of fun and frightful fairy tale insanity! I hope that you find them both thought-provoking and entertaining, and I thank you for taking the trip with me.

With greatest regards,
Jae El Foster

Welcome, dearies! My name is Madame Howell, and I am so glad ye have visited me today. I recently discovered an ancient book of fables and folk tales that has my hair rising straight up off my head! Perhaps ye would be intrigued by a story or two? In fact, there may very well be a Baker's Dozen full of 'em! Settle in awhile and I'll share these dark tales of mischief and mayhem with ye!

Comfy? Wonderful! I do hope ye have brought a blanket though, as this first tale will make yer blood run cold. Ye know how fairy tales often tell the story of true love and happily ever after? This story tells of true love lost and the repercussions of it that rippled throughout a kingdom. It is the story of a Queen who is no longer a believer in true love, and anyone who is... well, off with their head! This is A Heart Unfrozen.

A Heart Unfrozen

She ruled with a hand so heavy that it often crushed more than just her people's spirits. Within her kingdom, there was a fine line of tolerance and of rule. It was a *give and take* situation. The people gave, and Queen Estella took. The kingdom was not wealthy; she was not after their rubles or gold. She was after their hearts, and she stole them at every given opportunity.

To understand Queen Estella, one must understand a memory of her past that wrapped a black blanket of darkness around her soul, shrouding her from the pain and torment of love. As a young princess of seventeen, she had found her true love in the form of a neighboring kingdom's prince, but this affair was not to end well, as the neighboring kingdom was a rival of hers, and her father the King would not have such a betrayal as having his Princess betrothed to his enemy's son.

Upon vehemently ending their relationship, the King made Princess Estella vow to never see her love again. She agreed, but her agreement was woven as a lie, and behind her father's back, she continued to enjoy the company of her forbidden love.

She and her prince met in secret at any presented opportunity, even if those opportunities were few and far between. They often chose to meet at the lake or in the magical wildflower gardens that bloomed so colorfully throughout the countryside.

Every moment in his arms – every kiss that they shared – had made Princess Estella yearn for more from their relationship. She had wished to be his and for him to be hers, and she had prayed for their happily ever after.

One crisp winter night, when the land was covered with snow so white that it lit up the black sky with its glow, the Prince arrived at her castle, managing to slink past the guards and through the gate. Upon appearing at her window, he told her that he had scaled the three levels of rough castle stone, all the way up to her very room, on nothing more than the vines from dead ivy just to see her.

Princess Estella then threw herself into his arms – impressed and in awe at the idea of such a daring, romantic venture. He kissed her, and she felt as if she was lifted off the ground and sent to the heavens from it. When the kiss broke and she had taken a moment to gather her wits, she asked him what he was doing at her castle during the late hour – especially knowing how her father felt about him.

"I cannot take this separation anymore," he had told her in as hushed a tone as he could muster. "Gather yer things. Tonight, we depart this place on my horse. We will make a new home, somewhere far away from our battling fathers."

"Oh, my Prince," she told him, touching his cheek affectionately.

"My Princess," he replied as he returned the tender gesture, "my heart belongs to thee, for now and forever."

Once more, they kissed, and as their passion ignited into what should have been a moment of sensual bliss, the door to her room opened with startling force.

Two guards armed with swords then bolted into the room. They parted – one to each side of the threshold – and made way for the King to enter.

His entry was one that had filled Princess Estella with immediate doom. He was more angered at that moment than she'd ever witness; had he been any madder, she swore steam would have come out of his ears. He stampeded through the guards, stopping only a few feet away from his daughter and her forbidden lover.

"What is the meaning of this?" the King then demanded. His eyes were more frightening to the Princess than his words, but she stepped to him nonetheless, placing a barrier between him and the Prince.

"We are leaving here," she told him boldly, even as fear washed over her. "We are leaving tonight, and we shall live in peace – as far away from ye as we can get."

When she silenced, the King grunted – fuming. "How dare ye?" he then demanded and pushed his daughter aside, throwing her down to the floor. With a step, he drew his sword and swung it in front of him, severing the Prince's head in one clean swipe. The head bounced when it hit the floor and then rolled a few feet to the wall.

The Princess screamed until she fainted.

That night, when her father had returned to his room and slumbered soundly in his bed, Princess Estella slipped out of her chamber and into his. With the same sword that the King had used to kill the Prince, the Princess claimed her revenge. She severed the King's head in one swift thrust – just as he had done with the Prince – and when the dawn of the next morning arrived, she made witness of her kingdom as she held her father's head before the people in the center platform of the village square. It was there that she had pronounced herself Queen, and it was there that the new Queen implemented a new rule that changed the way true love was handled throughout her kingdom.

There simply was to be no true love allowed. There would be no courting or relationships. There would be no vows of marriage or the making of homes together. For as long as Queen Estella reigned, there would be no more heartache or hurt. There would be no more pain or loss – not through romance. Not through love. Love for a significant other was thenceforth proclaimed illegal and punishable by death.

Now, ten years into her reign, the Queen continued to mercilessly watch over the lives and intimacies of her people. The number of people within her kingdom had dwindled dramatically during her reign. Many had lost their heads from being caught 'in love.' Others lost their heads for becoming intimate with one another. There were a few who died simply because they wanted children to carry on their family name. Mating to impregnate was strictly prohibited throughout the kingdom unless it was between two assigned individuals under the strict watch and guidance of an appointed birthing maid. Under the Queen's command, six males and six females were chosen every six weeks and made to mate until insemination. Quite normally, the females were a mix of virgins and women suffering through their menstrual cycles, as the Queen's Royal Advisor had informed her that it was easiest for those two types of women to get pregnant.

Sex or intimacy, outside of arranged mating rituals, were punishable by death.

At the moment, the Queen sat upon her 'traveling throne' on the platform that stood as a political stage in the center of the village square. Two young lovebirds stood before her, each with a guard positioned behind them. They were guilty of kissing behind the castle and had been caught by Mathavious, Queen Estella's most entrusted guard.

"I see no use in debating this matter," the Queen said to the charged. "Ye shall lose yer heads. Guards!" She looked toward the uniformed men standing behind prisoners. "Take them to the chopping blocks!"

The executioner's chopping blocks sat several meters away from where the Queen was currently perched on the platform. Nearly everyone in the village was present for the event, as it was mandatory for many who were in attendance. The platform itself had been built in such a way that no matter how an execution was performed, it could in some way be seen by anyone and everyone, from presumably any angle.

As expected, the accused protested their sentencing, but Queen Estella had heard it all before. Every sob story – every excuse plausible. None were forgivable, as she had made blatantly clear over the years. Her rules were not to be broken, and those who did were subject to punishment.

The young man and his young female lover were forced down onto the chopping blocks, and one by one, the royal executioner silenced their pleas as he chopped off their heads.

Down to the audience, the heads rolled. For a moment, they stared up at the spectators and blinked repeatedly until their brains finally died. Then, their expressions went still – frozen in time.

"Would anyone else care to lose their head today?" Queen Estella asked in a loud and enthusiastic tone as she stood tall and prominently. "I would like enjoy my midday tea as quickly as possible, so please... do speak now if ye have done anything blatantly unforgiving. I will not be so kind and yer deaths will not be so swift if I find out someone is withholding their guilt."

The crowd was as feasibly quiet as it could be. She heard someone cough, but it was the executioner as he pulled the dead, headless bodies from the platform. Queen Estella smiled to him, even though he couldn't see her. He was one of her most faithful, she considered, and the royal executions would not have been so effortless without him in the position.

"Okay, then," she said when no one came forward to enjoy a beheading. "Carry on, peasants. Next week, twelve of ye will be chosen for the mating ritual, so prepare thy selves in advance."

The crowd began to mutter amongst themselves as they broke apart. The Queen took Mathavious's hand as he led her across the platform to the small wood steps down. Just as they reached the steps, they heard the voice of an old woman, shouting unlawfully.

"Yer frozen heart shall be melted," a haggard old woman yelled to Queen Estella, pointing a shaky finger at her. "Yer whole body shall be melted by the fiery hands of what ye have done!"

"What is going on here?" Queen Estella asked Mathavious. "Who is this insane old woman?"

"I have not seen her before now," the guard replied. "A hag from outside of this kingdom, most certainly."

"Get her out of here. Cut off her head if ye must."

"My pleasure," Mathavious told her and, smiling wide, drew his sword.

"I cast ye to yer hell, Estella the Heartless. I cast ye to yer sins!" the old hag continued as Mathavious approached her. "By the mighty hand of our dark lord Mephistopheles, ye an' all who follow ye shall suffer!"

"Enough with the banter, old woman," Mathavious told her

as he pulled his sword back. As he swung it, the hag opened both hands and pushed them forward. From her hands emitted a bright red light that encompassed the entire kingdom. Then, as the blade of the sword passed through her neck and severed her head, the light faded and the hag fell dead to the ground.

The powerful blast of light from the old hag's hands touched upon Mathavious as he beheaded her, and his body was flung backward. Against the platform, he landed with force – impaled through the heart by his own sword.

Those peasants who had not already fled began to panic, trampling over one another as they sought an escape from what they had just witnessed. However, there was a red and black shadow that began to cascade outside the stone archways and walls of the village square, surrounding it like an unearthly fog. Despite its sudden presence, Queen Estella watched in curious wonder as her people ran into it without heed. Once within it, she could not hear their uproarious screams anymore.

She thought, perhaps, this mysterious fog was feasting on her people, and as cold as Queen Estella had become, she was not quite cold enough to simply stand by and watch her citizens be slaughtered.

Moving back to her traveling throne, she stood before it and shouted loudly to her villagers. "Stop yer foolish scattering about!" she ordered and clapped her hands. "If ye go into that fog, ye shall die!"

It took them a moment, but the few dozen villagers that remained came to standstills. They looked at one another, at the fog that seemed to barricade them, and then at their queen. Despite what was happening, she smiled at them and sat.

"It appears that the hag has cursed our kingdom." Looking to Mathavious's dead body, she added, "She has also killed my commanding guard. This is an attack on our people – on our lives. If we step through the fog, we will die. So, we must simply wait this out."

"Wait it out?" she heard a villager shout in question. Another added, "For how long must we remain here?"

Once again, the people began to panic as they murmured their worst fears to one another. Queen Estella was no less afraid, she imagined, than they were, although she knew the importance of remaining poised and controlled. Taking a calming breath, she cleared her throat and relaxed in her throne.

"Unhand me!" came a shout from the darkness of the smoldering fog. Looking to her left, she saw them emerge – two headless peasants as they dragged her executioner behind them. Even though he fought against them, he could not free himself from their grip.

Even without their heads, Queen Estella recognized them as the two lovebirds that she'd had executed only minutes ago. Their heads were still on the ground, and when the undead creatures dragged the executioner to them, they retrieved the heads and set them back atop their necks. A red fire appeared at the points of incision, and like magic, their heads were fused back to their bodies.

With their heads reattached, the undead lovers looked at the executioner and removed his hooded mask. He, in turn, screamed from the horrific shock of what he was witnessing. Then, savagely, they began to tear at him until they had severed his head from his body – not giving him the mercy of swiftness as he had shown them. Facing Queen Estella, who watched with grim curiosity, the reanimated female tossed the executioner's head to her. It landed with a thump on the platform and rolled up to her feet.

Queen Estella looked down at it and stared into the executioner's eyes as he stared back. He blinked once and then died.

"Witchcraft!" a villager shouted from the thinned crowd.

"A curse from the hag!"

Bound in angst, the Queen looked to the hag's fallen body, only to discover that it wasn't there. Her ratty, tattered clothing was there, but otherwise, there was nothing but ashes. There were ashes with the clothing, and there were ashes where her head had landed.

"That was no hag," she whispered to her people, although she had intended her voice to be louder. "That was something much… darker."

Standing from her throne, Queen Estella kicked the

executioner's head away and looked all around her – peering into the black and red flickering fog that surrounded them just outside the walls of the village square. It was everywhere... everywhere but above and below them.

"What is happening, my Queen?" one of her villagers asked as she approached the platform. "What is this... strange fog that is surrounding us?"

"I do not know, but whatever ye do, do not wander out into it," Queen Estella informed her and then stepped from the platform, down beside her. "I fear that something horrid waits on the other side of it."

The peasant girl clutched her hands to her chest and stepped timidly away from the Queen, toward a group of villagers huddled near the far wall. "It is the Devil," she muttered in a skittish voice. "The Devil has come for us. He has come for us all..."

There was another scream. Screams seemed abundant today, the Queen thought as she turned toward the source. This scream came from one of her male peasants – a young man of around twenty who was screaming in terror at the body of Mathavious.

Headless, Mathavious was climbing to his feet amongst a puddle of his own crimson blood. Queen Estella observed with a slight of shock as her dead guard reached forward and grabbed the screaming peasant by his neck. As the young man fought against the grip, Mathavious ripped his head off and send it tumbling to the ground. A second later, he hoisted the peasant's corpse in the same direction; it landed only a foot or so away from the head.

Mathavious then turned toward his own head and retrieved it. Like with the two executed lovebirds, his head inexplicably fused itself back to his neck. When he looked at Queen Estella, she could see that his eyes had turned completely white. Looking to the reanimated lovers, she saw theirs were the same. Finally, she glanced at the executioner's body on the ground beside the lovers. It was beginning to stand.

"I demand an explanation for this!" the Queen shouted and took a step forward, toward the two she'd had beheaded. "Do not think for a moment that I won't chop yer heads off again – even if I have to do it myself."

Swiftly, she pulled her father's sword from its sheath at her side. Wielding it in front of her, she prepared herself for battle. Her eyes then went back to her commanding guard.

"That goes for ye too, Mathavious," she told him as he stared at her through orbs of white. "Thou hast served me well, but thou are now dead, and I prefer for the dead to stay that way."

Walking up to him, Mathavious stood waist high on Queen Estella from his position on the ground. With a clean cut, she severed her guard's head once more and watched it fall from his body. Keeping her eyes on Mathavious, she took a step back and let her jaw drop. Mathavious, seemingly unfazed by what she had done, simply bent down and retrieved his head. Once more, he placed it upon his neck where it once again fused and healed.

"What kind of Devil's magic did that old hag use?" she questioned, backing up as Mathavious climbed atop the platform in front of her. "Thou... thou should be dead, Mathavious." A bit unsteadily this time, she took another swing with the sword. This time, she chopped into Mathavious's neck, but she did not sever the head. Instead, it dangled from the neck and rested on his shoulder. There was no blood, but the Queen noticed a black puss that she hadn't observed prior, drizzling from the wound. Not even slightly dazed by the cut, Mathavious continued to take slow steps toward her.

Finally overwhelmed with fear and panic, Queen Estella dropped her sword and shrieked. Then, as she turned to run, she came face to face with the executioner, who had retrieved his head from where she had kicked it. On other side of her, the lovebirds approached. Four sets of white eyes burned terror into her soul as they cornered her, and as the Queen screamed for mercy and lowered down onto her knees, eight hands took hold of her and lifted her body over theirs, hoisting her into the air.

She fought against their grip and screamed for her release, but Queen Estella could not free herself from them as they carried her off the platform and down the village square. Her eyes grew wider as the frightening moment escalated and they carried her toward an archway and the red and black foggy smoke that lay behind it.

"No!" she begged, trying to squirm away. "Please! Please, do not take me into there! Please, unhand me!"

No matter how much she begged or fought, she was no match for the unearthly hold that the four reanimated corpses had on her. Her scream was high-pitched as they carried her into the fog, and once she was inside of it, her scream silenced – even though it continued to come from her body. There was no sound here in this fog – only thick stillness with high humidity and thin air.

"Please, let me go!" she tried to say, but even though her lips moved, no words came out.

They carried Queen Estella like this for minutes... maybe hours – perhaps it was even days. The scenery never changed. It stayed black and red fog, and all concept of time had been lost.

Finally, up ahead, she saw a red glow – circular in shape and growing larger in size with each passing step that they carried her. It was bright, but it was light in this dark and mysterious fog, and that meant it was a way out perhaps, or a way to... somewhere.

Through the red light, they stepped, and a few steps in, they lowered Queen Estella to a stone ground that felt hot to the touch. She tried to stand, but Mathavious put a hand upon her shoulder, pushing her back to her knees. There, she remained as she looked around frightfully at the hellish world around her. A glance behind her showed that the red-lit portal that they had crossed through was gone. An entrance back into the fog was nowhere to be seen.

Instead of fog, instead of the village or anything else in her kingdom, Queen Estella was surrounded by burning embers, steaming coal, volcanic eruptions, and rivers of lava. It all seemed almost like it was contained within a cave – as if underground – and yet it seemed to have no tunnels or exits. There were shadows – hundreds of them – that played tricks with her eyes, moving all around and through things as if they were intentionally taunting her. Before her, she saw a stone platform rise up from the ground. It was not unlike her platform on the village square, but it was darker and more daunting.

From the center of the platform rose a throne. This land's version of her 'traveling throne,' she imagined. It was shaped similarly to hers, but it was made of black iron instead of gold and was bejeweled in rubies instead of diamonds and sapphires. Finally, atop the throne, a man materialized. He was handsome and young, and he was dressed as a king in the black and red shades of his kingdom. He sat tall and proud, fit with a smile upon his face. His eyes were charming, and his expression almost put Queen Estella at ease.

"Even here, in my abyss, ye look ravishing, Queen Estella," the young King began. His words struck a bone of flattery. "However, ye are here on trial."

"On trial?" the Queen asked, appalled. "Who dare accuse

me of a crime? I am the Queen of my people. My rule is law."

"Ye are accused of having a frozen heart, Queen Estella," he told her plainly. Extending his left hand, the old hag from the village materialized like a ghost. The Queen's eyes gaped in confusion. "Yer accuser – Queen Esmeralda of the Harkenship Kingdom."

Staring into the old Queen's eyes, Queen Estella felt her heart sink. She knew that family name. She knew that kingdom. Her accuser – a woman she had thought no more than a wicked hag – was the mother of her fallen prince.

"I – I did not kill yer son...!" she defended through emotions that threatened their own release. "I *avenged* yer son by slaying my father with the same sword he had used on the Prince." Tears filled her eyes as she was forced to remember what had happened and what she'd had to do. "I *loved* yer son..."

"Thou art accused of having a frozen heart – not murdering the Prince of Harkenship," the young King corrected. "Thou art accused, however, of murdering the witnesses to yer left and yer right."

Looking to either side of her, Queen Estella watched in horrific shock as the spirits of those she'd had executed during her reign materialized. They each stood still with their heads in their hands, watching her through white, dead eyes.

"No!" she shrieked, fighting off the tears that wanted to emerge. She would not cry. No... she was stronger than that. She had to be strong. Whatever was happening right now, it was not the moment for weakness. "I rule justly!" she defended with a shout once she'd calmed her breathing. "Each of these damned souls is guilty of violating a law, and they were well aware of the punishment before breaking that law."

"Ye got yer heart broken, so no one can be happy and in love?" the King questioned. He stood from his throne and crossed the platform toward her. At the edge of it, he kneeled down and looked into her eyes. His eyes flickered with fire. "I see no use in debating this matter." He was using her own words from earlier, and it chilled her bones, despite the unbearable heat all around her. "I find ye guilty of both murder and vengeance from a frozen heart. The punishment for each is quite different."

"What is the punishment for murder?" she asked him and then glanced around at the ghostly decapitated figures around her.

"Ye shall lose yer head," he said bluntly.

Queen Estella swallowed down a knot in her throat and closed her eyes. Somehow, she knew that was what this man would say. Opening her eyes, she nodded and looked at him again. "And the punishment for vengeance from a frozen heart?"

"Why... yer heart must be unfrozen, of course." Standing upright, he looked at Mathavious, the royal executioner, and the two lovebirds that had carried her into this pit. "Guards, take her to the chopping block."

"No!" she screamed hoarsely but loudly as the four

reanimated beings yanked her from her knees and began to drag her across the ground. "No! Let me go!" she pleaded, crying out in horror as they pulled her across burning embers and patches of molten fire.

The chopping block was not on the platform here like it was in her kingdom. Here, it was a large stone slab near a river of lava, and Queen Estella was placed atop it. The four pinned her down as the young King approached.

"Who are *ye* to decide *my* fate?" she asked him and spat as he approached. Her spit evaporated in the air before it ever had a chance to reach him.

"My fair Queen," he told her in a kind tone as he brushed her cheek with the back of his hand. She noticed his hand was hairy and his nails were long, thick and black. His touch made her tremble. "I am Mephistopheles, and thou art in *my* kingdom now." Turning toward Queen Esmeralda, he gestured to her. "Thou shouldst have become a champion for love when yer love cost Queen Esmeralda her only son." Looking back at Queen Estella, he added, "Instead, ye made her son's death into a more horrible tragedy than it began as, for ye continued in yer father's footsteps, slaying all who broke yer rules by falling in love. Ye didst not avenge the Prince. No, fair Queen. Ye turned his legacy into a nightmare and his family name into a whisper of fear. For that, Queen Esmeralda has traded me the gift of her eternal servitude in exchange for ye."

"This… this has to be a mistake!" Queen Estella argued. Her expression twisted further to terror as she caught a glimpse of Mephistopheles's clawed hand approaching her. "Certainly, we can make amends…!"

"The first step to making amends," he told her as he reached for her chest, "is to thaw yer frozen heart."

She screamed more loudly than she ever could have imagined as Mephistopheles dug into her chest with his razor-sharp claw, breaking through bone and tearing through tissue as he reached for her heart. The pain was unbearable – excruciating… She felt like her entire body was on fire. Almost paralyzed from shock, she watched as the hand pulled up and out of her, reemerging with her heart clenched in it.

Her heart was, indeed, frozen. It was bluish white and had ice crystals all over. As it beat, the ice crystals rattled ever so slightly.

"There is only one way to thaw a frozen heart such as yers," Mephistopheles continued, and with a pitch, he flung her heart into the river of lava.

"No!" Queen Estella screamed and pleaded, but it was done. Her heart was not only thawed, but now it was melted. As the paralysis and panic began to fully encompass her, she wondered how long she would continue living without a heart to pump the cold blood that ran through her veins.

"Is that not better?" Mephistopheles asked, looking down at

her with a smile. His fangs were pearly white. "Do ye not feel like a great weight has been lifted from yer shoulders? Dost thou not feel more pure?"

He was insane, she realized – this Mephistopheles. He was reveling in her fear and feeding off of her pain. She could see it in his demonic yet hypnotic eyes and the smile on his face. Mephistopheles truly loved his position of power.

For that and that alone, Queen Estella felt a tinge of respect for him.

"Now," he whispered as he stood up straight and stepped back, "do not get upset please, although ye *are* about to lose yer head."

He laughed the most horrifying laugh that Queen Estella had ever heard. She couldn't understand why she wasn't dead yet – why her body was still functioning after her heart had been ripped from her. And yet, here she was, primed and ready for her beheading.

"Please…" she begged, one more time, "this is all a misunderstanding."

"Here," Mephistopheles said to Queen Estella's executioner as he handed her what appeared to be her father's sword. "Ye do it."

The executioner took the sword. The Queen watched him as he approached. His face was emotionless, although it was unusual for her to see him yield a weapon without his masked hood on. With the hood, he had been her servant. Without it, he was no more than the corpse instructed to kill her.

"No…" she told him as he raised the sword above her neck. "Ye do not want to kill me. I – I have always been good to ye. Please… please, spare me."

The executioner didn't as much as flinch as his queen pleaded with him. Once she was done, he lowered the sword with heavy swiftness, slicing through her neck and severing her head completely. It was a skill of his that Queen Estella had been most proud of, and she had gotten to experience it firsthand.

As the executioner stepped aside, Mephistopheles approached the slab once more. He looked down at Queen Estella's body and the blood from the slice. Then, he looked at her head. Amazingly, her crown was still pristinely in place. He took the crown from her and tossed it into the river to melt. Then, grabbing a fistful of her hair, he raised Queen Estella's face to his.

She stared him in the eyes, unsure of how this was possible. Without a heart… without a body… somehow, she was still alive – able to see and hear and think and smell. She could even feel the pull as he held her by the hair.

Deciding to chance it, she opened her mouth to speak. Much to her amazement, her words came out.

"How… how is this possible?" she questioned, blinking in shock at her assailant.

Mephistopheles's smile grew. He carried her with him as

he walked. "Ye'd be amazed at what all's possible," he answered and stopped walking. Angling Queen Estella's head, he pointed her face toward an iron birdcage. With a bit of gentleness, Mephistopheles placed her head inside the cage and shut its small door. "Welcome to Hell."

Lifting the cage, he carried it over to Queen Esmeralda and handed it to her.

"I believe this belongs to ye," he told her as she took the cage. "I think yer assignment for a while shall be to ensure that our fair Queen Estella understands that this is, indeed, Hell."

With a demented laugh that frightened her, Mephistopheles dematerialized and Queen Estella was left alone with her slain lover's demented mother.

Queen Esmeralda turned the cage in her hands so that the two were face to face.

"Ye think ye've had tha' worst of it?" the haggard Queen asked her. Her smile was near toothless and grim. "Aye, now... tha' fun 'as yet to begin!" She cackled like a witch as she set the cage down atop a tallish stone and opened the door. Taking the head out, she held it before her. "What say we begin by trimmin' off some o' that fat on yer nose, eh?"

"What?" Queen Estella asked, terrified of the notion. "What are ye talking about?"

Instead of a reply, she received more pain as Queen Esmeralda began to use the nail of her index finger to carve a new nose from her old one. Queen Estella's screams rang throughout the bowels of hell like music to Mephistopheles's ears – a music that continued to harmoniously ring for the extent of an eternity.

Well, now! Wasn't that just a lovely story? Don't worry, friends. It was only the tip of an incredibly cold iceberg, I vow to thee.

From a Queen with a heart of ice to a lonely maiden in search of her only friend, our next story will have ye take caution the next time ye consider wandering into the woods at night. It is about a young woman whose only companion is her beloved cat. When she fears her cat lost, she ventures out into the enchanted forest – a place unsafe for her or her cat at night.

There be times when all seems hopeless, dearies. In those times, it could be wise to trust in the kindness of strangers, even when ye have been warned against it. At other times, one might reconsider. Such is the case in The Dark Changeling.

The Dark Changeling

Once upon a time, there was a young, poor maiden named Rosette without any family or a human friend to keep her company. She had but one companion, a cat named Tucker who lived with her in her small cabin in the woods. Fearful of the many dangers that lurked in the surrounding woods, Rosette kept Tucker indoors at all times. There were predators beyond these drafty, rickety cabin walls – predators that would have eaten poor Tucker as a snack or a small meal.

By the warmth of a fire within a wood-burning stove, Rosette sat in her comfortable-enough chair with her feline friend atop her lap. Tucker was a short-haired, blondish orange cat who loved having his belly scratched, his chin tickled, and the bridge of his nose stroked. He purred heavily with each bit of attention Rosette showed him, and every now and then when she would pull her hand away, he'd paw at her and mew for more.

"Oh, yer such a loving rascal," she told him as she scratched behind his ear. He purred his usual contented response. "I'm so fortunate to have a companion like you. Why, without thou, I'd likely go crazy in this cabin all alone. Tucker, please don't ever leave me."

Tucker purred and nuzzled against her, leading Rosette to believe he understood every word she'd said. She smiled and continued to scratch and pet him until she felt like she would fall fast asleep in her chair. She jolted upright as her consciousness began to drift. Tucker sensed her sudden alertness and leapt from her lap. Lazily, he walked to the stove and lay down before it.

Rosette stood and stretched with a yawn. Then, she ambled to the front door and opened it, stepping out. Outside, she lit a small torch and used it to light two larger ones thirteen meters from the cabin. The light from these flames would keep the woodland demons away as she slept.

Back inside, she closed the door behind her and changed for bed. She climbed beneath her covers and blew out the candle at her bedside. Only when she was just about asleep did she realize that her precious Tucker had not joined her.

"Tucker!" she called, lifting her head from the pillow. "Come to bed!" She waited a patient moment, but Tucker did not join her. This was quite unlike the cat, as he usually curled up at her feet the second she was under the covers. "Tucker!"

She began to grow worried for her favorite feline, and with a toss of the covers, she was back on her feet and headed to the stove where she'd last seen him. Tucker was not there. She felt her nerves turn frantic with angst, and hurriedly, she searched the small cabin from top to bottom. Her companion was nowhere to be found.

A horrible fear swept over her as she worried that her cat had somehow gotten outside. Was it possible that he'd raced out with her when she'd lit the torches? Had she been so careless as to leave the door open while doing this task?

Hurriedly, she went to the door and opened it. Her ears were filled with the sounds of the woods. Insects, animals, owls, serpents and drudge monsters... There was the cackling of a wench demon echoing from somewhere far away, but not too far away. Her fear for poor Tucker grew.

She walked to the edge of the clearing and stood between the two bright flaming torches.

"Tucker!" she cried out, hoping he would hear and race to her. "Tucker, where are ye?" When he didn't show, she called out for him again. Her only responses came from the sinister sounds of the forest creatures.

She knew if she was to find her precious Tucker, she would have to step beyond the safety of the torches. This made her nervous, as the woods were the most dangerous in the dark. Still, Tucker was her best friend – her *only* friend – and he was faithful to her. She owed it to him to seek him out and find him. Now, all she needed was the bravery to do so.

Rosette stepped back inside her small cabin and put on her green hooded cloak for warmth and to shield the sight of her flesh from predators. She took with her a lantern, although this lantern – unlike the two at the foot of her property – would provide no safety to her, only light.

The only weapon she had to take with her was an axe, but

she was hesitant to bring it. With a lantern in one hand and an ax in the other, she'd have no way to carry Tucker back with her. The axe had to stay behind, which meant Rosette would have to venture out into the woods with no protection.

Stepping back outside, she secured the door behind her and marched forward. Once again, she paused between the two great glowing torches. She wished she could take them along with her – they were enchanted and kept the predators at bay. However, she would have to push on without them, or else leave poor Tucker out there to fend for himself.

"Tucker!" she cried out once more before stepping forward and away from the torches, leaving her sanctuary behind.

The light from the torches lit her way for a good bit, but soon, she was shrouded in the darkness of the night and the shadows of the woods. She was nervous, scared, and anxious – anxious for the safety of her companion, and anxious to make it back to her cabin alive. The further she walked, the louder the sounds of the woods became. Aside from the sounds of the animals and insects, she heard the other-language whispers of the demons and the cackling of the dreaded imps.

"Tucker!" she yelled, wishing she didn't have to speak at all, but if her cat was somewhere out there, she had to yell for him to hear her and know where she was. "Tucker, come back! Please, Tucker!"

"I can be yer Tucker…" she heard a slithery voice say to

her, and Rosette froze in her steps. With the light of her lantern, she looked all around for the source, but saw no one or nothing.

Perhaps, she thought, her ears were playing tricks on her. These woods had a way of fooling the mind. Trickery from ancient demons, she knew, was a ploy to lead the unsuspecting into traps. Rosette was not an unsuspecting woman. She was quite aware of the many horrors that lived in these woods. She expected to encounter everything and anything that one should never have expected to encounter in the woods.

She ignored the voice and moved on. A few paces ahead, she stopped and called out Tucker's name. Once more, she received a reply in the same slithery voice as before.

"I can be yer Tucker," the voice said again. It came from behind her now instead of in front. The words were accompanied by the sound of a rustling. Turning around, she watched the leaves on a bush quiver.

"Who's there?" she demanded and held her lantern out toward the bush. Even though she was nervous – incredibly fearful – she stood straight and held the light steady. "Show thy self!"

Rosette watched the quivering bush as whatever was hidden within it moved about. Then, after a moment, she saw a golden serpent slither out. Once from under the bush, the serpent stood on its four small clawed feet and smiled up at her. Its eyes were red; its nose, nothing but two thin slits. Its smile was fanged and unpleasant.

"A serpent..." she muttered and took a frightened step back.

"I can be a serpent," the creature told her and then lifted upright onto its hind feet. "I can be Tucker."

"Tucker is a cat!" she spat, offended by the insinuation that this creature could pose as her beloved Tucker.

"I can be a cat," the serpent replied. "I can be anything ye want me to be."

Rosette trembled and gasped. She nearly lost her grip on the lantern as she took another step away from the creature.

"Yer not a serpent at all," she told it and looked at it through hard eyes.

"I am a serpent right now," the creature said. Then, while standing upright, his form began to change. Right before Rosette's eyes, he became a golden feline – furry and vibrant. A fluffy thick tail grew from his backside, and whiskers shot out from beside the pink button nose that replaced his slits. His red eyes remained. "I can be yer Tucker the Cat."

"A changeling!" she gasped and put her hand to her chest. "Stay – stay away from me!"

The changeling licked his paw in the manner that a cat would and then smiled at her through its small fanged mouth.

"Would ye rather I become something else?" Right before her eyes, the changeling became the most handsome man that Rosette could have imagined, with the exception of the slanted red eyes and fanged smile. "Ye prefer this form, yes?"

"I – I want to find Tucker… *my* Tucker," she answered with a trembling voice. As she ended her sentence, a wolf howled loudly from somewhere in the distance.

"Yer Tucker is food for the beasts by now," the changeling said in its slithery tone. Then, it turned back into a cat. "I will be yer new Tucker. Ye can pet me and scratch my belly, and I will rest atop yer lap and make pleasant, contented sounds." The creature tried to purr, but it was nothing like Tucker's purr. It was, instead, much darker and more demonic. Rosette shivered upon hearing it. The purr was absolutely frightening.

She turned and left the changeling behind, not offering it another word of reply. For a long moment, she walked in the cool darkness – the light of her lantern helping her navigate through the forest. Twice more, she called out for her dear cat, but the little feline neither replied nor showed. On a third shout of his name, she nearly leapt out of her skin as she heard the changeling's slithery voice reply.

"I can be yer Tucker," it said, repeating what it'd told her before.

"Go away!" she shouted, turning to face the changeling, which was in its serpent form again. "I do not want thou to be my cat!"

"Ye need a companion?" it questioned with a sly grin. "Maybe someone to talk to?" Suddenly, it manifested itself into a new form – the form of a young woman around Rosette's age. "I can be yer companion."

She was becoming exasperated by the creature. The hour was growing later, and she had to find Tucker and return home before she became some hungry beast's supper. "Go back to yer faeries," she commanded of the creature. "Ye may not pose as a substitute for my Tucker or for anyone *else* in my life, for all that matters."

Rosette once again walked away, but the changeling continued to follow. His presence was pestering her, and she wanted to be left in peace during her search for Tucker.

"I have been banished by my faeries," it told her as it turned into its serpent form again. Despite its smallish size, it managed to keep pace with her. "They say I am bad. That I am a poor changeling. They say that I am too eager to please and that I talk much too much."

"Yer faeries are wise," she said and snorted.

"I was a young boy recently," it continued. "They swapped me with a real boy in the village – one that was bright and plump and happy, their favorite kind to feed on. My new parents noticed I wasn't their real boy, but I told them I was their boy now – that they're *real* boy had been eaten by the faeries and they'd given me as a replacement." The changeling sighed and then shifted into the form of the boy it had switched places with. Rosette grunted when she noticed and then nervously averted her eyes. "I didn't mean to tell the parents what had happened, and they took the news poorly... banishing me from their home and sending out a hunting party to find and kill the faeries."

"Seeing as thou has been banished," Rosette noticed, "I suppose they didn't find the faeries."

"No, they found them." The changeling smiled. "The faeries ate every last one of them."

Rosette gulped and trembled. "I'll hear no more of such things. I have a cat to find."

"Ah, yes... Tucker. I can be yer Tucker." With as much boyish charm as possible, the changeling smiled. The grin was still sharply fanged. "Let me be yer Tucker."

"Ye are *being* a thorn in my side, changeling." She huffed and began to walk faster. Despite her best efforts to lose it, the changeling kept pace.

Above, storm clouds grew and took over the night with heavy rumbles of thunder and the brightest flash of lightning that illuminated the woods before her. While the world was lit, she caught the quickest glimpse of a wolf, just a few meters ahead of her. The wolf – brooding and on the prowl – noticed her also. When the world was dark again, she heard it snarl.

Holding her lantern high in front of her, she heard the snarling growl of the wolf grow as it neared her. She saw the wolf again as it stepped toward her, and as it opened its mouth and leapt toward her, she screamed and braced herself for death.

There was another sound – another snarl and growl. When she wasn't tackled savagely to the ground, she opened her eyes to see a second wolf attacking the one that was about to devour her. She watched as this golden wolf tore into the assailant, ripping at its jugular with its sharp fangs and tearing into its flesh with fierce claws. There was little struggle from the other wolf, as it was grounded and defeated – assisted into the land of the dead.

"Changeling?" she asked, breathing heavily as she held the light closer to it for a better look.

The changeling's snout was red; blood ran from its fangs and stained its paws. It looked at her and smiled a familiar grin.

"He was going to eat thou," the changeling said as it turned back into the golden serpent on four clawed feet. Slowly, it half-slithered, half-ambled toward a nest of bushes. "I shall leave ye to yer hunt."

Even though the changeling's voice was still slithery like a serpent's, Rosette detected a hint of sadness in it. She watched the creature disappear into the bushes.

Standing there, she considered it for a moment. While she was seeking her beloved feline Tucker, she was also in mortal peril, defenseless in the woods. The changeling had just risked its life to save hers, even though she'd made every effort to shoo it away. Rosette began to feel a tinge of sympathy for it, and she crouched down toward the ground.

"I suppose I could at least let ye accompany me as I travel

through these woods," she told the creature. Softly, she offered a hint of a smile.

From the bushes, the changeling's head protruded. Its red slanty eyes were wide with excitement. A gigantic smile covered its face. "Really? I may accompany ye? Shall I… shall I turn into a wolf again and help defend ye?" Fully working its way out of the woods, the changeling stood on its hind legs and shouted, "Roar!" while beating its tiny clawed fists against its golden scaly chest.

Rosette laughed. "Only if another wolf should try to eat me. Until then, ye may remain in yer normal form."

The changeling seemed puzzled at first. "My true form does not sicken ye?"

She looked at him with hard, studying eyes and took in every inch of his serpent form. Then, she smiled. "No. I admit I was shocked by yer appearance at first, but now I find ye quite remarkable. I do not find ye sickening at all."

This was encouraging to the changeling, and for the rest of Rosette's venture through the woods, it stayed right by her side – loyal and faithful, guarding her against any of the predators that lurked in the darkness. However, they ended up empty-handed when it came to finding Tucker. The cat was gone – lost to the woods or in the pit of some monster's belly.

Rosette was distressed over this, but she was thankful to have a new companion at her side as she ambled back home. When they reached the edge of her property and the two lighted torches that stood to protect it, Rosette continued on toward the cabin but the changeling came to a halt.

Noticing it was no longer at her side, she looked back at it and asked, "Are ye coming?"

The changeling looked at the torches and shook its diamond-shaped head. "I cannot pass through here. The torches are enchanted and the land is protected against creatures like me." Once again, the changeling sounded sad as it spoke, and Rosette felt herself bubbling over with sympathy for her new friend.

To show the changeling that he was welcome, she extinguished the torches and let it enter onto her grounds. Giddily, it followed alongside as she walked to the front door and opened it. She held the door open for the changeling, and once it was inside, she shut it tight.

Just then, she heard a familiar mew come from the top of her bookshelves. Looking up, she saw Tucker, safe and sound, resting atop the books and dust.

"Tucker!" she exclaimed and stepped toward him. He mewed again and leapt from the shelving and onto the floor.

Before Rosette had the chance to scoop her favorite feline up into her arms, the changeling took notice of him and attacked. Rosette screamed as she watched the creature swiftly kill her cat, and just as swiftly eat it.

With a blood-covered mouth, the changeling looked at her and asked with a smile, "I can be yer Tucker now?"

I suppose if yer cat be missing, ye should look everywhere before setting off in a hunt for it, eh? What a wonderful story that was, and how exciting that the friendly changeling may have found a home. I certainly enjoy a happy ending. Don't ye?

This next tale evokes true happiness, as it takes place in one of my favorite settings – a castle's dungeon. Once again, the thought of true love takes its toll when a handsome Prince is turned to stone and a broken-hearted young woman is sentenced as the villain and made to reside in a dungeon. Personally, I find dungeons quite comfortable. They're cool and moist, and they be dark enough to catch a good nap in. For some reason, the young woman in this tale is eager to be Rescued from the Dungeon.

Rescued from the Dungeon

"If ye scream, I shall sew yer mouth shut," the man told her as he locked the heavy iron door between them. She stared at him through the bars; darkness shrouded all but his grim smile. "Ye will suffer for what ye have done, witch." He spat at her and laughed, and then disappeared into the darkness.

Lady Anna Bellum was frightened, cold, and hungry. She was also innocent of the charges against her, but the King believed differently. She had taken a liking to his majesty's son, Prince Farwell of Lancaster, but he had not held the same feelings for her. Lady Anna Bellum had not taken this news well when he delivered it to her on the village square, and she had fled to her home in tears, crying herself to sleep atop her bed. When she awoke the next morning, she felt a bit better, but Prince Farwell did not. In the night, he had magically transformed into stone while slumbering in his bed.

The King was swift to blame Lady Anna Bellum, insisting that she was a witch and had placed his son under some horrible spell. She simply hadn't done a thing, but no one would believe her – not the King or his Queen… not even those in attendance when she was brought before the royal figureheads. She was banished to the dungeon, where she would remain unless she admitted to being a witch and used her powers to restore Prince Farwell.

That was an impossible task. Lady Anna Bellum had no magical powers whatsoever. She was pretty and she was energetic, but that was it. Otherwise, she was average – like any other prominent lady from a well-to-do household.

"Curse these castle walls," she muttered as she slumped down and rested against one of those walls. "Curse whoever put me here."

A rat scuttled nearby, squeaking as it hunted for food. Lady Anna Bellum squealed and pulled away, inching into the crevice of a nearby corner. She did not want to become its supper.

From outside these dank and crumbling dungeon walls, she heard a downpour of rain. Shortly thereafter, water began to drip from all around. A steady stream of it began to come down right atop her head, forcing her from her corner.

She heard the rat squeak again. This time, Lady Anna Bellum rushed to the cell door and pressed her back against it.

"Why so frightened?" the rat asked her in a voice as understandable as her own. Lady Anna Bellum screamed. "If ye keep screaming, ye will alert the guard. Do ye want that man to return?"

She silenced and considered the words. No, she did not want the guard to return – not unless he was doing so to feed or free her… or to save her from the talking rat. She then considered that she was going mad. No rat spoke in human language. They squeaked and squealed, but that was about it.

"I've gone mad... absolutely mad," she muttered to herself as she watched the rat approach. Even as dark as it was in the cell, she could see the whites of his eyes and pointy little teeth.

"Ye be thinking yer crazy," the rat informed her, "but ye be sane as the day is bright."

"How would I know the day is bright?" she asked. "I'm locked away in a cell in a dungeon. There is no day here."

"They think yer a witch," the rat continued. "They think yer responsible for the transformation of the Prince."

Lady Anna Bellum nodded. "Yes... but I am innocent. I have no magical abilities. They won't hear my alibi either. They insist I am to blame."

"But *we* know better, do we not?" the gray creature asked. His whiskers twitched with every spoken word. "Surely, no one would blame ye if ye simply walked out of here."

Lady Anna Bellum looked at the rat long and hard. Then, she bluntly laughed at the creature. "Perhaps ye be the one who has gone mad," she told him. He looked at her with his beady eyes. "One, yer *speaking* to me, which I know that rats cannot do. Secondly, ye think I can just walk through these iron bars or these stone walls? If I could do that, I would *surely* be a witch."

"But we know ye are not a witch," the rat concluded.

"So I cannot leave."

The rat smiled up at her and winked. Lady Anna Bellum had never seen a rodent wink before. It was unnerving. "If ye have a yearning for adventure, fair maiden, perhaps I can be of assistance."

In the distance, down the long dark hallways beyond her cell door, Lady Anna Bellum heard voices that grew nearer with every word. She jerked her head toward that direction.

"Ye should hide out of sight," she said and looked back to the rat. It was nowhere to be seen. Then again, in this dark cell, it was easy for such a creature to disappear.

"She *will* confess!" she heard a familiar voice shout. Instantly, she recognized it as the voice of the King. "She will confess by sunrise and restore my son, or she will be burned at the stake!"

Lady Anna Bellum swallowed nervously and took a few steps to a corner, hoping to hide in its shadows.

"I still say the lady don't look like any witch I've ever seen," she heard the guard tell the King.

"Are ye questioning my authority?" The tone of the King's voice was more than intimidating. It was downright threatening.

"No, sire!" she heard the guard squeak. "I'd never do such a thing!"

The King huffed and, soon, Lady Anna Bellum saw him standing at her cell door. His appearance was intimidating. His eyes searched the cell briefly, but he quickly caught her stare in his.

"Stand before me, witch!" he shouted and pointed down to

the ground before him. "I command thee!" As if needing to emphasize the matter further, he stomped his heavy foot to the ground.

Lady Anna Bellum trembled. Slowly though unsteadily, she stood upright and slunk toward him, barely moving through each step. Still, it was not a far walk, and all too quickly, she stood before the king – only the iron bars of the cell door separating them.

The King looked her over and grunted. Then, holding his chin high, he looked down on her as if she was nothing more than a lowly servant instead of the Lady of Rosehip Manor.

"I demand ye restore my son to his rightful form!" he insisted in a heavy, firm tone.

Lady Anna Bellum considered her words, and she wondered if she should dare speak at all. Then, with a jittery jaw, she said, "I have told ye that I am no witch."

The King sneered and he trembled, likely from his rage. "Ye have until sunrise, *witch*, to confess yer crimes, or else, ye shall be burned." With a huff, he turned around and stormed away from her cell. The guard followed closely behind, holding a lighted torch to guide their way.

In a moment, the light from the torch faded from Lady Anna Bellum's view.

She waited a bit longer before screaming – hoping the King was far enough away to not hear her. Then, once her fit was silenced, there was nothing more to be heard than her heavy breathing and the dripping of the rain water.

…And the rat.

"So, they plan to burn ye," the rat said, startling Lady Anna Bellum and bringing yet another shout from her lips. "That's certainly a pity, I dare say."

"Why will the King not listen to me?" Lady Anna Bellum fretted and began to pace. She was no longer afraid of the strange talking rat. In fact, she now believed that she was imagining him. "I have insisted over and over again that I am no witch!"

She was becoming angry. Her pacing motion quickened. The rat began to pace with her, scurrying along with her steps as if they were out walking a winding trail together.

"Things will change," she muttered, pausing in her steps. "Things will be better in the morning. Once everyone has rested, I will be able to convince the King that he is mistaken. He will release me and everything will be fine."

The rat laughed in an unnatural way. "Ye wish to convince the *King* that he was wrong?" As his sentence ended, the rodent burst into a second bout of heavy laughter. "That's – that's the most *naïve* thing I have ever heard!"

She looked at the rat sternly, even though a part of her knew he was right. The King was *never* wrong, and those who questioned his authority or judgments often met their fate at the end of a rope hanging at the gallows.

"I have heard," the rat continued once his laughter ended, "that they take the bones of burned witches and grind them down to dust, to prevent them from coming back."

Lady Anna Bellum shivered at the thought of it. She'd heard of the atrocities and abuses of power within the kingdom. She'd even witnessed the hanging of a poor man who had stolen bread to feed his family. Still, she'd never been the one on the receiving side of this. Now, as she found herself in that situation, she didn't know what to do or if she could survive it.

The rat went to the far wall of the cell and clawed against it. "Ye can be free. Ye can leave this place."

The lady released a loud 'hah' and grimaced at him. "For a figment of my imagination, ye certainly be hard-headed, rat."

"A figment...?" the rat asked. His tone was offended. "Lady, I am as real as thee. If ye don't believe me, perhaps scratch my head."

She cocked an eyebrow. "Scratch yer head? Like a dog?" The idea of scratching a rodent on the head appalled her and she folded her arms in protest.

"No... like a rat," he clarified. "I am much too small to be a dog, m'lady."

Lady Anna Bellum half-smiled at his rather humorous reply. "Whimsical rodent, aren't ye?"

"I have my moments." He smiled in that peculiar way again. "So, what say we get out of here, or would ye still rather try the King's temper come sunrise?"

She looked around her as she considered her options. There was no way she could see out of this cell, aside from the door that she had no way of opening. Still, she felt she should humor her imaginary friend. Perhaps if she played along, he too would see that there's no way for her to leave. Only then would he quit pestering her about it.

"Sure," she told him, looking at him again. "What have I to lose? Let us leave this place, rat. Show me how."

"For thee, beautiful Lady Anna Bellum, it is my honor."

Once more the rat smiled, and Lady Anna Bellum smiled back, challengingly. Then, the rat came close to her and, at her feet, he looked up at her and spoke words she did not understand. In a sudden and breathtaking way, she felt her body shrink and change. This moment of change was brief, and she gasped to find that she was now face to face with the rat. It was then that she realized he had turned her into one.

"What have ye done to me?" she asked, frightened by the mystical transformation.

"I have made it possible for ye to escape," he told her. "Now, follow me!"

He turned from her and darted to the cell door. Paralyzed from the shock, she stared at him for a moment. He easily passed through the iron bars to the other side of the cell. Lady Anna Bellum mustered up some courage and followed behind, exiting the cell through the same spot as the rat.

"I don't believe it," she exclaimed in a fast breath once she was out. "I'm – I'm out of the cell."

"Now, to get ye out of this dungeon completely," the rat replied. "Just stay beside me and ye shall soon be reunited with yer freedom."

Freedom... the word sounded like the most precious thing as it swam through her thoughts.

"How is this possible?" she asked as she followed the rat down the long and winding, damp and dark hallway. As hard as she tried, she couldn't fathom the fact that she was now a rat and making her escape from her prison.

The rat didn't respond. Instead, he led her through a 'rat hole' in the stone wall near the stairs. It was darker and wetter here, but the stench wasn't nearly as rancid as her cell had been.

"We're almost there," he finally said and picked up his pace. Lady Anna Bellum picked up hers also, as to not fall behind. "Be prepared for a drop. Roll when ye hit."

"What?" she asked, hoping he hadn't really said what she thought she'd just heard. Then, before he even had a chance to respond, she watched him drop out of sight. She tried to slow her run and stop, but there was no opportunity to do so. She, too, quickly began to fall as the ground disappeared from beneath her.

The fall was a short one though and she landed with a thump that she swore bruised her backside. She tried to follow the rat's advice and roll, but she bounced instead.

For a moment, everything was still and quiet. Then, she heard the distinct chirping of crickets all around. Looking behind her, she stared up at the massive castle from which she'd just escaped. She gasped, and then sucked in a breath of fresh air.

"I – I just cannot believe it!" she exclaimed, excited over her newfound freedom. "Thank ye ever so much!"

Lady Anna Bellum turned to face her rat friend, but in the darkness of the night and the thickness of the grass, she could not see him.

Then, several feet away, she saw a rustling in the grass. Lady Bellum's eyes stretched wide as she watched the rat transform into a tall and handsome man. His kind eyes looked down at her, and through smiling lips, he recited more words that she could not understand. She then transformed into her regular human form.

"Ye are not a rat at all," she whispered to the man, who must have stood six feet at least. He had beautiful golden hair that fell in long locks and cascaded around his shoulders and neck. His eyes were bright and, even in the dark of night, their blueness was stunning.

"And neither are ye," he told her with the kindest voice she'd ever heard. "At least, not anymore." He smiled coyly and winked.

"Please, tell me yer name, and tell me how any of this is

possible?" Lady Anna Bellum begged of him.

"My name is Lord Charles of Ravenstone Manor," he explained, "and while ye may not be a witch, there are those of us who are." His smile broadened. Plainly, he added, "The males of our species prefer to be known as warlocks or wizards."

She wanted to challenge that he was a wizard, but he'd already proven his powers to her. Instead, Lady Anna Bellum asked, "Are ye responsible for Prince Farwell's current stone state?"

Lord Charles beamed brightly. "I couldn't help myself, Lady Anna Bellum. After witnessing how cruelly he treated ye on the village square, I couldn't let him go unpunished."

She gasped and put a hand to her heart. "Ye saw that?"

"Aye," he acknowledged. "It was a heartless move on his part to treat a lovely maiden as thee in such a cold way. He showed that he had a heart of stone, and so I made the rest of him match it." He chuckled a bit and Lady Anna Bellum felt her smile widen.

"Ye did that... for me?" she asked. She simply couldn't believe that such a powerful man as Lord Charles had taken the time to help a stranger such as her.

Lord Charles nodded lightly. "Ye be the most beautiful woman I have ever laid eyes on. It pained me to watch a man treat ye so cruelly. Prince Farwell was undeserving of yer love. Now, ye have yer freedom, and the Prince shall never treat another lady with such disregard again."

It was, by far, the most romantic thing that Lady Anna Bellum had ever heard, and she swooned from it. Then, she once again felt her mind and body riddle with fear. Looking down to the grassy ground, she felt her body flush.

"What is wrong?" Lord Charles asked. She looked at him and saw the concern in his eyes.

"I *am* free," she told him, "but for how long? It is only a matter of time before the King and his guards notice I am missing from my cell. They will hunt me down like game in a forest, and when they find me, I shall surely be burned."

"I can protect thee, fair lady," he replied. "I can ensure the King and his men bring ye no further peril."

He turned to face the castle and whispered another enchantment. As he did, he waved his hand before the massive structure. Lady Anna Bellum watched, but she could see no change once the spell was complete.

She didn't know what she'd expected. Perhaps she'd thought the castle would simply disappear, or maybe it would crumble to dust. Instead, it stood tall and mighty, just as it had been before.

"What did ye do?" she asked the lord.

"I turned everybody within the castle walls to stone, of course," he said merrily. Lady Anna Bellum's expression lightened, as did her mood. It was the most gallant thing anyone had ever done for her. "Here," he said, offering her his hand, "let us leave this place."

"And go where?" she questioned, accepting his hand in hers.

"Wherever we want to go."

Hand in hand, the two left the castle behind them, walking toward the morning's rising sun.

Perhaps a happily ever after is a splendid thing after all, at least if yer not turned to stone by a wizard after vengeance. What a lovely story that was! I'll have to think twice next time before I grab a random rat to toss into my brew. A human in a rat's disguise could ruin the flavor completely...

Time in a dungeon can pass ever so slowly, but there are mystical powers that can manipulate time itself. A young Princess is about to discover this very principle when she wanders too far from her castle and must take shelter in the enchanted forest. Who knows what her future holds when she awakens Within the Hollow Tree.

Within the Hollow Tree

While wandering through the enchanted forest, Princess Camilla sought a place to rest. She was a long way from her beloved castle, but only because she had become lost. She'd only intended to go out for a stroll, but she became scattered in her thoughts and somehow lost her way.

The forest was genuinely beautiful, but as the sun began to set, she found it to be eerie and intimidating. When the daylight had shown, it had been magical and inviting. She hadn't counted on being in it at night, and she wished she'd paid more attention to where she had walked.

"Oh," she fretted as she looked at the dark and looming trees around her, "all I wish for is somewhere to rest my eyes. Surely, when morning comes, I shall be able to find my way back home. Father and Mother must be terribly worried by now."

Her royal parents had often warned her never to stray too far from the castle grounds. Always, Princess Camilla had listened and obeyed. She would have done so this day as well, had she not been so distracted.

There was a chill in the air and she shivered from it. An autumn breeze accompanied the chill, and she knew she had to seek shelter or she would shiver unpleasantly throughout the night. Yet, it was getting darker by the moment, making it more difficult for her to see. She'd called out for help a few times, but no one had heard her plea. If they had, an answer had been refused.

Once more, she cried out as loudly as she could, beckoning for someone to rescue her from her miserable state. "Anyone, please!" she shouted as mightily as she could. "Help me! I am lost and cold!"

Again, her call went unanswered.

Princess Camilla had twice thought to turn around and retrace her steps, but she had not walked along a path, nor had she paid any attention to her surroundings. At night, her chances of making it back to her castle were unlikely. She had no choice but to wait it out until daylight and then try to find her home again, but doing so without shelter to protect her from the cold breeze was something she wasn't sure she could bear.

Alas, she continued her journey until the sky was black and the forest seemed even darker. She came to a large tree upon which she decided to rest beside. As she lay against it, she discovered it had a large opening, and that the tree was hollow.

This tree was her best chance for protection from the cold, she decided, and after feeling around inside it for a moment to ensure there was nothing there that could harm her, she climbed inside of it and sat in a crouched position. It was much warmer inside of the tree, as the breeze pushed around it but not inside of it. Exhausted from her walk and her dismal anxiety over being lost, the Princess closed her eyes and went to sleep.

Throughout her slumber, she had the worst dreams that made her whimper and cry out. She dreamed of great wars, bloodshed, and death. She dreamed of her family's kingdom being overtaken – her parents, overthrown. Princess Camilla dreamed of great burnings, devastation, and new beginnings. The beginnings were of the sort that she neither understood nor would have been able to fathom while awake.

"Ye shall be forever lost," came a voice from somewhere around. In her dream, she could not see the speaker, but the voice was as present as if it was from directly in front of her. "Ye shall have no home."

Princess Camilla awoke with a start. She sat up quickly, knocking her head on part of the hollow tree's insides. Squinting, she looked through the large hole and saw that daylight had come. She hurriedly stepped out onto the soil of the enchanted forest.

With a sigh, she took a deep breath of fresh air, smelling the morning dew. She also smelled flowers… springtime flowers. She found this scent unusual, considering the time of year.

"How strange…" she muttered and then stretched and yawned. "My imagination must be reacting to that horrible dream."

Yet, when the Princess looked around, she saw that her nose had not betrayed her. There were wondrous springtime flowers blossoming everywhere, and the trees had fresh new leaves, when just last night they had been nearly bare.

She knew this was an impossibility that was far beyond

actual impossible. She'd simply taken shelter in the tree for a rest; how could spring have come already? Turning around, Princess Camilla stared up at the massive hollow tree that she'd slept in. Her eyes widened with further surprise.

Aside from already having new leaves upon its branches, the tree and its opening appeared much larger than it seemed last night. She gave some credit to the fact that it had been dark when she reached it and that had made it impossible to fully tell its size. Yet, she knew the size of the opening and how she'd had to climb into it. She knew how much space had been there for her when she'd settled down for sleep. Now, the space was quite a bit larger than it had been, and the tree practically towered up to the heavens.

It also did not look like any other tree around. Its bark was as black as a crow, and its leaves were glowing pink and purple. Never before had she seen such a tree, and she gasped in amazement at its sight. The tree looked ancient – as old as time, she presumed. The Princess looked from it to the other trees around – many of them also reached great heights that seemed much more than they were last night.

"It is what I get for wandering around in the dark," she said and shrugged it off. Then, she reached atop her head to adjust her tiara before trying to make her way back home. It was not there, when she knew it had been there when wandering through the enchanted forest just yesterday. Looking down to the ground, she saw it at the foot of the tree, covered in vines and dirt. Only a portion of it stuck out, and when she pulled it free, she noticed that it looked greatly aged and had lost its shine. "How strange…" she muttered and put it atop her head nonetheless. "I really must have it polished when I make my way back to the castle."

She turned away from the tree and headed in the direction from which she came. The walk was long and tiring, and nothing looked familiar to her – even areas that she knew she must have passed through when walking yesterday. She came to a clearing that she somewhat recognized, but there were more trees in it than before – tall trees that looked like they'd been around for decades. Above her, a soaring noise disturbed the silent tranquility around her, and Princess Camilla looked up toward its source. There in the sky was something she related to a bird, but it was unlike any bird she'd ever seen. It appeared to be made of some sort of shiny material and, from what she could tell, it had no feathers at all. Behind it, it left a trail of dusty smoke that dissipated as it continued onward.

While the sight of the flying object gave her chills, it encouraged her to move onward toward home. She entered back into the thick of the forest – much thicker than she remembered it – and had to struggle to climb over fallen trees, overgrown shrubs, and prickly vines that she hadn't come across yesterday. On one of these vines, the Princess ripped the hem of her dress, but she couldn't worry with that right now. She'd have the royal seamstress repair it when she made it home.

Minutes turned to hours and she began to grow tired again. Her body ached from the walk, and she was hungry and thirsty. Finally, up ahead, she saw daylight breaking through the trees, and she knew she was close to home. When she reached the edge of the forest, she noticed a path just beyond it that she'd never seen before. In fact, she'd never seen anything like it. It was not a path made of dirt, but it was instead made of something hard like stone. Yet, it was seamless – unlike a pebbled walkway would have been. Gray in coloring and perfectly flat, she found it curious and rather frightening. Crouching down beside it, she hesitantly put a hand to it and touched it. It was warm from the sun but it did not harm her.

She stood upright again and took another step forward, walking onto the unusual path. It did not feel like a trap; nothing bad was happening to her. She stood there for a moment, looking down at it, when all of the sudden she heard a monstrous sound coming from behind. Turning around, she saw a beast of a creature speeding toward her. It was large and steel, moving on wheels with tremendous speed and not a horse to guide or pull it. The creature made a sound that reminded her of the honking of a goose, and as it neared her, it veered to her right and sped on beyond her. Stunned, the Princess turned her head so that her eyes could follow it. Out of the right side, a human's head appeared and shouted an obscenity at her while waving a fist in the air.

"Watch where you're going, lady!" the person yelled. Then, their head disappeared back into the contraption.

"Lady...?" she muttered as she tried to overcome the shock of what she saw. "I'm a *Princess*..."

In that moment, Princess Camilla decided this unusual path was not safe for her to stand on. Hurriedly, she crossed it and went to the grass on the other side. The first thing she noticed here was a large fountain in a clearing where, just yesterday, no such thing had existed. She wondered if she'd come out through a different part of the forest, but over the trees beyond the clearing she could see the peaks of her castle. Curiously, she walked to the fountain and took a closer look.

It was made of shiny marble with a mermaid atop the base and pool. The mermaid was lovely, but water came from her mouth, continuously spilling down into the pool. There was a gold plaque at the base that read: *The Goddess Atargatis, c. 1000 BC.*

"Surely, father would have told me if he was having such a structure created," the Princess mused. "But he knows of my love of mermaids... perhaps it's meant to be a gift to me."

The sight of the fountain lifted the Princess's spirits and she started toward the castle, eager to thank the King for the gift and to apologize for ruining what was obviously meant to be a surprise. The fountain overjoyed her, and she found her steps quickening as she crossed the clearing to the small layers of trees that surrounded the back of her castle home.

At the foot of those trees, she discovered more unusual sites. There were benches made of wood and steel, a gazebo that resembled them, and a gate just beyond those. The gate was closed and attached to a fence that seemed to go on in both directions for a good length. None of these things had been here before, she realized, but she put her hand to the gate and pushed it nonetheless. It opened for her, and the Princess stepped through.

When she reached the castle, she reached the side of it first and noticed the age on its stone and brick. The castle was no more than fifty years old, built for her grandfather before her father was born. Yet, it looked much older than that now. Perhaps it was simply weathered, and there was a good chance that she just hadn't noticed it. After all, she spent most of her time inside the castle, and when she was outside, she just wanted to wander the grounds and enjoy herself.

At the front of the castle, she noticed the entrance had been updated. The large grand doors had been replaced with similar doors that were not quite as grand. There was no longer a lush purple and gold carpet leading up to it, as was custom for when it wasn't raining, and no guards stood at the entrance. Instead, there was a sign that claimed the castle was closed.

"Closed?" she questioned and became further confused. "How could my home be closed?"

There was a knob on one of the doors and she reached for it and twisted. Despite what the sign said, the door pushed open easily. It was much lighter than the old doors, and for that much, she was thankful.

Inside, it was like her parents had instructed the place to be fully redecorated, and all in a day's time. Nothing looked the same, and in areas, there were red velvet ropes blocking off access to certain rooms and stairs. All around, not a soul could be seen, but at the far end of the room above the fireplace, she saw a portrait of a King. It was not her father, however, and she began to worry.

"Hello?" she asked loudly as panic began to swarm within her. "Hello? Mumsy? Father?"

"Hello?" the Princess heard a woman respond from a room that was behind one of the velvet ropes. It was not the voice of her mother, nor did it sound like any of the servants she was acquainted with. "Who's there? We're closed until tomorrow morning."

The Princess swallowed and neared the velvet rope. When she reached it, she answered with, "It is I, Princess Camilla. What is going on here? Where are my parents?"

"You're *who*?" the woman in the other room asked. Then, the Princess heard her mutter, "I swear... all the crazies seem to show up when *I'm* here... All I want to do is finish this bookkeeping and go home."

Finally, Princess Camilla saw her step from a room. She was wearing a simple black dress with a strand of pearls around her neck. Her hair was gray and curly, and she wore glasses atop her button nose. She looked grandmotherly, and seemed warm in appearance.

"Well…" the old woman said as she approached the Princess and the velvet rope separating them. "Don't you look *festive*, young lady?"

"Festive?" the Princess asked. "My tiara is in need of polishing and my dress is tattered. How, might I ask ye, doth this be festive?"

The woman looked her over and sneered. "You do look like you've been through the wringer alright," she noted. "You should probably go on home now and clean up. We open at nine tomorrow if you'd like a tour."

Princess Camilla cocked an eyebrow at the woman's strange and casual way of speaking – especially when directing someone of her royal status. She folder her arms and huffed. "I *am* home… although it doesn't look much like my home anymore." She looked around and took in her surroundings again. The rooms were the same, but the furnishings were different. "I demand to see my parents at once."

The old woman laughed. "It's just you, me, and the dust," she said through her chuckle. "I'm sure wherever your parents are, they're worried sick over you."

"My father is the *King* of this castle!" she shouted. "King Artemis the Third. My mother is Queen Pricilla."

The old woman's smile faded. "I'm afraid you must be confused, dear girl. Why… King Artemis has been dead for nearly three hundred years now. Queen Pricilla died long before him, suffering from a sleepless depression when their daughter suddenly disappeared."

While Princess Camilla understood the woman's words, she could not fathom what they meant. She'd been gone for only a day and a night – not three hundred years. Everything she was being told was impossible, and she refused to be made a fool of.

"I _am_ Princess Camilla, and my parents were here just yesterday – alive and well," she said adamantly and stomped her foot for emphasis. "How dare ye question this?"

"Now, calm down, young lady," the woman began, but before she said any more, she looked at the tiara on the Princess's head. Her eyes grew wide. "Where... where did you get that crown?"

"It is _my_ crown," she told her strongly. "It is my birthright to wear it!"

"It – it has King Artemis's royal insignia," the old woman noted. "It would have certainly belonged to the royal princess... but that's – that's impossible." Her eyes left the tiara and returned to meet with Princess Camilla's. Then, she began to study her face. The color seemed to fade from her. "Can... can you wait right here for a moment?" she asked in a tone that showed nervousness.

The Princess said nothing and held her strong stance as the woman retreated to the room she'd been in. When she returned, she held in her arms a large and heavy-looking book. The woman set the book down on a nearby table and began to flip through the pages. When she reached what she was looking for, she stared at it for a long moment and then shifted her gaze back to Princess Camilla.

"It's... uncanny," she whispered. "Unbelievable."

"What is unbelievable? That I am who I say I am? I assure ye, I have no reason to lie."

The woman picked the book up and carried it to the Princess. She showed her the image on the page, pointing to it. "This is the last known painting of Princess Camilla," she began, shuddering as she spoke. "The actual painting has been lost to time, I'm afraid... but my dear... the resemblance is striking."

"It should be," the Princess said as she looked at the image. "It *is* I."

"But that would mean that you're over three hundred years old, child," the woman noted and looked the Princess up and down once more. "That simply cannot be."

Over three hundred years old... Princess Camilla thought. It was all too surreal – too unbelievable to be true. How had she fallen asleep one night and awakened over three hundred years later? All of a sudden, the Princess's head was spinning. She considered the possibility that this was just another dream... that she was still asleep within the hollow tree, but she knew it wasn't so. She was awake, and she was no longer in the time that was her own.

"Perhaps you would like some tea, dearie," the old woman

said, stirring her from her thoughts. Princess Camilla looked at her blankly. "Something to calm you. I will put on a kettle and be right back."

She watched the woman walk away, leaving the book on the table. When she was out of her vision, Princess Camilla turned around and studied the place she once called home. It felt like home no longer. Things had changed – drastically – and she needed to get away from this place; she needed to get back to the hollow tree where this all began.

In her haste to leave, she snatched the large book from the table and then hurried to the door. Once outside, she ran with the book clutched to her until she was far from the castle's entrance. She stopped briefly to catch her breath and turned around, taking one final look at the place she had been born and raised.

Across the unusual gray path, she ran and plunged into the enchanted forest. She hoped upon all wishes that she would be able to find the tree that had somehow sent her here, but she knew it would not be easy. The sun was setting again, and she had to make haste.

When it was dark, she slowed her steps and walked more cautiously, but she remembered certain areas she had passed through before – areas that she'd found overgrown and unusual. Finally, her wishes and prayers were answered as she came to the tree with the opening large enough for a person. When she reached it, she stopped and felt the opening, unable to see much more than blackness. With one hand grazing the tree, she circled it – something she had not done when she woke up. The tree proved to be incredibly thick, and on its back side, she found another hollowed opening.

"Perhaps," she thought as she stood before it, "if I climb into this side and fall asleep, I shall awaken in my own time once again."

It was her only hope, and with the great book clutched to her, she climbed into the second opening of the tree and sat. There, she closed her eyes and focused solely on falling asleep.

When she awoke, it was morning again. She opened her eyes to the daylight coming through the hollow tree's opening and smiled down at the book in her hands. If it held all of the history that the old woman in the castle had told her about, perhaps she would be able to warn her parents of their future and prevent her father from being overthrown. Perhaps by returning to her own time, she would be able to keep her mother from entering into the deep sadness that was said to bring about her death.

With a newfound excitement and a sense of urgency, Princess Camilla climbed out of the hollow tree, discovering it to be smaller than when she awoke yesterday. This was a good sign. Yet, this good sign came with other signs that did not feel quite so good. For instance, all of the other trees around her were small – saplings – and the forest seemed quite bare to how it had been two days ago.

Giving this little more thought, the Princess clutched the book close to her and began her venture home. When she reached the opening from the forest, she found that the strange gray path was no longer there. It was grassy all around. She crossed through to the clearing where a fountain had been, but the tribute to Atargatis was also gone. There were no benches, no gazebo, and no fences or gates. Astoundingly and much to her despair, there was also no castle or small wooded area that would have separated it from the clearing.

She realized then that the back side of the hollow tree had indeed transported her into the past, but it wasn't her past. It was a past far before the time when she left – a past in which she didn't even exist in. She wept for a long while with her face pressed against the book until her eyes ran out of tears. Then, she returned to the hollow tree and climbed back into the opening that had taken her to the future. Princess Camilla decided that she would try again – and again… and again – forever more until she finally found her own time and her home… *if* the hollow tree so granted it to her.

I once knew a young girl who lived in a hollow tree. I wonder if this hollow tree was hers. After all, it has been a while since I have heard from her…

Children can certainly be a handful, but they can also be a blessing. Sometimes, they can even be just a wish that the bearer hopes to come true. Wishes are often costly things when granted, but in this next tale, there is a mother who is willing to pay any price. What will happen in The Goblin and the Baby? Read on, dearie, and discover.

The Goblin and the Baby

There once was a beautiful castle that sat atop a land lush in greenery, flowers, and trees of all sorts. The castle was ruled by a wonderful King and Queen, who treated those under their rule with love and kindness. Never was there conflict within the kingdom, and never was there war with neighboring kingdoms. There was no need for such, as peace was practiced throughout this King's land, making it an idyllic place to live.

The King and Queen had hopes of having a child to carry on their name and to one day take the throne. After several years of trying and hoping, their wish went unfulfilled. Try as they did to keep smiles upon their faces, they were growing older and they knew the time for having a baby would someday pass.

Against her husband's knowledge, the Queen set out one night, atop a horse and cloaked in disguise. She rode the horse into the surrounding forest, where she'd once heard a great witch resided. The Queen had never seen this witch with her own eyes, but she believed the rumors to be true, as those in her kingdom had no reason to ever tell a lie.

Slowly, she and her horse sought through the forest, seeking a cottage or a cabin or some sort of small dwelling that a witch might have resided in. After hours of this, the Queen began to grow weary of her quest and considered it was time to return to the castle. As she began to turn her horse around, a glow of a small fire caught her eye.

The Queen climbed down from her horse and tied his rein to a tree. With soft steps, she approached the fire. When she was near it enough to see better, she noticed a silhouette dancing around it. Immediately, the Queen knew she had found her witch. She smiled nervously, cleared her throat, and stepped closer to the fire.

For a long moment, she remained silent, observing the woman as she danced freely around the fire. The woman was bare of clothes and had long white hair that fell below her breasts and swayed with her motions. She couldn't quite make out her facial features, but through the flickering glow of the fire, she saw that she was old.

She had not heard anything at first but the roar of the fire and the rustling of the leaves around her. Then, she picked up the faint whispering of the witch as she chanted a mantra the Queen could not understand. It was an intriguing sight to behold, and she had no fear while observing it. The Queen was a brave and strong woman who'd never once in forty years of life found a reason to be afraid. Thusly, being in the presence of an old witch in the middle of the woods, naked and dancing around a fire while chanting ancient words, did not disturb her.

When the witch silenced and came to a stop, the Queen stepped from the shadows and lightly applauded. "That was lovely," she told the haggard woman. Seeing her stilled gave the Queen a greater knowledge of her features; the woman looked beyond old and nearly like a mummy.

With one eye closed and one eye bulging, the witch looked at the Queen and took a startled step back.

"Please, do not be alarmed," the Queen said in a soft and pleasant tone. "I mean ye no harm. In fact, I have come from my kingdom in search of thee."

With her bulging eye, the witch studied her for a moment, as if unsure what was going on. Then, through a slim smile and crooked teeth, she asked, "Ye seek *me*?"

"Oh, yes!" the Queen exclaimed and took a step nearer. "My name is Queen Gloria of the Kingdom of Pleasantville. I have come in need of yer help."

This seemed to shock the witch even further, and she took another step back. "Ye seek my *help*?" she asked in her crackly voice. "I live here, in these woods, *because* of yer kingdom!"

The Queen's eyes grew in surprise. She had no idea what the old woman was talking about, as she'd only known of the witch through myth and rumor. "Please, I am afraid I do not understand... What does ye living in these woods have to do with Pleasantville?"

The witch sneered at her and then looked to her side, down at the dirt ground. There, she spat and then looked back at the Queen. "This be where ye banished me to," she told her with bitterness melting off her words. "O'er a century ago…"

This news came as a surprise to Queen Gloria. She'd never once heard of the witch living within her kingdom, nor had she heard of a witch ever having been *banished*. She'd never seen record of this event either, and her kingdom was well documented by the village historians.

"I – I have never heard of this," she admitted in a somber but dumbfounded tone. "How could I not know of this… this *atrocity*?"

"Ye surely wasn't even a glimmer in yer mum's eye," the witch told her as she looked the Queen over. "What ye be? Fifty?"

The Queen raised an eyebrow. "Forty," she said, flatly.

The old crone snickered. "If ye say so…" She hobbled her way around the fire and neared the Queen. The Queen was tempted to take a step backward but decided against it. "Ye say ye need my help? What is it ye wish of me?"

The Queen smiled again, feeling relief that the witch was willing to hear her plea, despite the supposed travesty that had happened between the crone and her kingdom long ago. "I – I wish to have a baby. A namesake for my husband. We have tried for so long, and I feel like our time is running out."

The old witch smiled. Then, a slight and low cackle followed. Rubbing her hands together, the witch took another step nearer and looked up into the Queen's wide and wondering eyes.

"So," the witch began, "ye wish to have a baby… a boy, at

that!" She cackled again.

"Oh, yes!" the Queen acknowledged. "A beautiful baby boy! Oh, it would be so wonderful, ye understand. He would continue this great time of peace throughout our kingdom for another generation."

The witch snickered again, but it seemed a bit unpleasant to the Queen.

"Time of peace..." the old woman mumbled. "Beautiful baby boy..." She grumbled for a moment and looked at the fire. Then, facing the Queen again, she instructed, "Remove yer clothing."

The Queen gasped. "Excuse me?"

"I shall give ye yer baby," the witch explained, "but ye must be a part of the ritual for the spell to take effect."

"I – I have to dance naked around the fire?" the Queen asked.

"Nay," said the witch. "Ye must lay atop the large stone at the foot of it, with yer legs open toward it. I shall handle the rest... but it shall come at a *cost*."

The Queen eyed her queerly. After a moment of consideration, she asked, "What kind of cost?"

The old witched rubbed her hands together once more. "Ye shall have yer baby, but once he be born, ye shall reward me with the item of greatest value within yer kingdom."

Again, the queen took a moment to consider the proposal.

The most valued item in her kingdom was the fire diamond that had belonged to a former King, who long ago ripped the jewel from a dragon's chest. It had been in the kingdom for centuries, and it was certainly one of the most prized objects in the world. But, for the sake of the kingdom's peaceful state and to have a child of her very own, Queen Gloria was willing to wage it.

"Ye have a deal, witch," she told her and smiled. Then, per the witch's orders, she undressed and lay down naked atop the cold hard slab. She'd thought it would have been warm, due to its nearness to the fire. Instead, it felt like ice.

The witch began to chant something Queen Gloria did not understand. Then, she began to vibrate and shimmy, flailing madly about. The Queen closed her eyes and suddenly began to feel incredibly warm. The warmth soon began to burn, and as she opened her eyes and looked, she saw the old witch standing in the middle of the fire, chanting and shaking but not burning. The fire was coming up through her body and then washing over the Queen.

Queen Gloria began to scream. The witch began to chant more loudly, and the fire's warmth flooded her and invaded her womb, planting its mystical seed.

All at once, everything came to a standstill. The fire died away completely. The witch stood still and quiet, and Queen Gloria felt cold again, with the exception of her womb. It was incredibly warm.

"It is done," the witch told her and stepped from the smoking embers within the fire pit. "Leave this place an' do not return. In nine months, ye shall deliver to me the most valued item in yer kingdom. I shall send to ye a goblin in the night. Ye shall give the goblin what he has come for. Until he receives it, he shall not leave. Should ye decide against fulfilling yer end o' our bargain, he will wreak havoc throughout yer kingdom, and the precious *peace* ye have come to know and love will be no more."

Confident in her ability to keep her end of the bargain, the Queen assured the witch, "Have ye no fear, dear witch. I shall pay thy price."

Although Queen Gloria had never encountered a goblin before, she most certainly didn't want to risk angering one. Her kingdom's peaceful existence was at stake, and she would do anything it took to assure its continuation.

"We shall see," the old crone told her. "Now, be gone from here."

The Queen, dressed and once again concealed in her cloak, unhitched her horse and hopped atop him, riding him swiftly back to the castle. She entered unnoticed the same way that she had left, and in her room, she climbed in bed beside her King. She then awoke him from his slumber and allowed him to ravage her.

She did not tell the King of her encounter with the witch in the woods. She let him believe that her pregnancy was a true creation between the two of them, and it was celebrated throughout the kingdom. Word of the pregnancy quickly spread through neighboring kingdoms, and visitors from near and far came to show their excitement for the upcoming child.

On the sixth day of her ninth month, Queen Gloria felt a sudden fire fill her womb. It was a much more intense heat than the blissful warmth she'd felt throughout the pregnancy. When her water broke, lava spilled out onto her birthing bed. The King watched in amazement at her side, and the Priest began to pray. Finally, the child was birthed and presented to his parents.

The King screamed in shock and stumbled backward to the wall. The priest fell to his knees, hoping to strengthen his prayers, and the midwife fainted. The doula stepped back after presenting the baby and crossed herself.

Queen Gloria held her swaddled child in her arms and marveled at him. He had fiery tresses of golden hair, big flickering eyes, and the most adorable smile she'd ever seen. He giggled at her; smoke escaped with his breath. Then, he pointed a finger up at her. It was then that the Queen noticed all of his fingers – and when she looked, his toes – were fire diamonds. They wiggled, bent, and moved around like the fingers of a normal baby, but they were pure fire diamonds and bound to his flesh and bone.

The twenty little fire diamond appendages, she realized, now made her child the most valuable item in the kingdom. This felt intentional. She believed the witch had tricked her and planned for this very thing to happen, and the realization of this was both devastating and angering.

Queen Gloria had never felt either of these emotions, and she didn't care one bit for them.

"What have ye done?" the King asked her. She looked up into his frightened blue eyes. "That – that is no child o' mine."

"Oh, but it is," the Queen told him as she stroked the baby's fiery hair. Its touch didn't burn her a bit. "This is our baby boy… yer namesake and heir to the throne."

There was a rumbling from outside the castle. The King went to the window and looked. A shocked gasp escaped him. "Oh, my beloved… what *have* ye done?" He repeated the question from before, but this time it was more heavily laden in dread than shock.

"What shall we do, sire?" the Priest asked, joining him at the window.

"Seal off all entrances to the castle. Whatever happens, we cannot let that goblin in here."

So, she thought, the goblin had arrived – just moments after the birth of the child. She thought of how cruel that was of the witch, to allow her a measly moment with her baby and then to snatch him away from her. She wouldn't hear of it. Witch or no witch, Gloria was the Queen of this kingdom, and she would not allow her baby to be taken.

Panic soon erupted within the castle. She heard the commotion from the floors below, and she noticed her husband flee from the birthing chamber, along with everyone else. She, however, could not tear her eyes away from those of her newborn son.

"I shan't let anything hurt thee," she told him as she stroked his fiery hair. Then, she stood from the bed with him and cradled him as she walked to the bookcase. She pulled one of the books to her and the case spun outward halfway, opening up to a secret chamber. Once inside this chamber, she pulled on another book, which pulled the book on the other side back into place and closed the secret door.

The Queen moved swiftly through this dark chamber, but she managed well even if she'd brought no light to guide her way. There were stairs going up and down at the end of this space. She chose to go down, assuming the goblin would work his way up the castle in search of the valuable child.

Holding her baby close to her bosom, she traveled down as far as the steps would lead her and entered into another secret hallway, cut off from the rest of the castle. This hall went on for quite a bit before it opened up into a large space. Queen Gloria had been in this secret space only twice before – once with her husband, and once alone as she'd sought a way to pass some time.

There was a wooden table in this space near the center of the room. She found it and placed the swaddled child atop it. Then, she sought for a lantern. There were a few here and there, and she found one with little trouble and lit it. Its kerosene-ignited glow dimly filled the space.

"I shall let no harm come to thee," she promised her child, returning to his side. "The forest hag gifted ye with yer treasures and spectacular features as a trick to steal ye away from me. I shan't let her win. Ye shall remain here with me, safe and free from her wicked clutches."

The child looked up at her with bright, flaming eyes. He smiled and giggled. Then, he burped a breath of fire. The Queen marveled at her son's gas.

Even as deep beneath the castle as they were, she could still hear the rampage happening above her. The faint echoes of screams... the crashing of walls and doors... Briefly, Queen Gloria wondered if any of them would survive – her beloved King included. But she understood that none of them truly mattered, as long as the heir to the throne survived this goblin's massacre. If the King were to perish, she would rule in his place until their son became of a governing age, and then she would proudly step to his side as he took the throne. Together, they would work to restore whatever peace the goblin interrupts.

The child began to cry and she worried that he had indigestion. He could burn the whole forest down with belches like his, she thought. Taking him in her arms once more, she cradled him and bounced him and kissed his warm forehead. His tears subsided once he felt secure in his mother's arms.

"We shall wait it out," she told him sweetly. "The goblin

ive enough, and we shall be free to leave this cold chamber."

Her words were only meant to comfort. She remembered what the old witch had told her once the ceremony was complete. She'd vowed that the goblin would not stop his rampage until he had the most valuable thing in the kingdom in his hands. The Queen hugged her baby tight. He nuzzled into her milky bosom.

There was only one thing to do, she decided, and that was to flee the kingdom. By the witch's own words, the trade was for the most valuable item within the kingdom. If she carried her son outside of the sanctity of Pleasantville, he would surely be safe.

Once they were out of the castle, they could take her horse to a neighboring kingdom and seek royal assistance. The problem was getting out of the castle. There was no exit here, except a door that opened up to an underground tunnel she had never explored. If it led to a dead end and the goblin found them there, they would surely be doomed. The only other exits were above, where the creature was likely tearing its way from room to room in search of the newborn.

She decided to chance the tunnel. She went to the door and opened it, and holding her lantern in one hand and her child with the other, she stepped through. She set the lantern down long enough to close the old heavy door behind her. Then, she set forward on her path and began to walk through the unknown.

The tunnel was carved through the dirt and rock, and dust

kicked up with every step she took, making her path even harder to see. It also curved every few meters, winding around large chunks of cut rock and slate. Eventually, she saw the dim pink light of a sunset from up ahead and felt relief wash over her.

Her pace quickened as she approached the tunnel's exit. The light grew brighter; the opening, larger. As she reached it, she came to a stop and looked down. Had she taken one more step, she and her child would have stepped off the end of the land and plummeted down to the rocky sea below.

Queen Gloria took a frightened step back. She began to tremble. From far behind, she could hear the gargled snarls and grunts of the goblin. He'd discovered her secret hideaway and her tunnel. It was her child's scent, she knew, that had led the beast to her. How else could he have tracked her to this underground trap?

Turning around, she aimed the lantern straight ahead and saw the growing shadow of the goblin as he neared her. The goblin came into the light and stopped. It gazed at her and at the baby she held close in her arm. The Queen, in turn, shrieked from the goblin's unsightly appearance.

He was large – quite large and gruesomely built – with a hump in his back that caused him to lurch over. His head jutted out from between his shoulders on a thick and stubby neck, and his knuckles dragged the ground. He was blue in coloring with black age spots all over. On his bulbous nose was a wart nearly the size of the Queen's fist. A strand of slime dangled from one nostril and slapped against his dry and chapped lips. In his hand, he held a spiked club that was covered in blood and flesh.

"The treasure," he said in a grim, almost drunken growl, "if ye please."

"No!" Queen Gloria exclaimed and held her son closer. She took a step backward, nearer the dangerous ledge. "The witch shall never have *my* son."

The goblin looked her over. Drool from his fanged mouth slipped to the ground, dampening it in slime. "Ye shall die then, wench."

"Wench?" she exclaimed, offended. "I am the *Queen* of this kingdom."

"Ye *were* the Queen," he corrected. "Now, ye be fish bait."

The goblin took a large and heavy step forward. He swung the club at her head, but as she lurched back, he missed. Queen Gloria lost her footing in that moment and she fell backward, leaving the ledge with her child in her arms. A scream bellowed from her as they tumbled down to the rocky sea.

Queen Gloria died when her head hit a jagged rock. The water took the precious newborn, sweeping him away from his beloved mother. Its currents washed him onto a murky bank nearby, where a wise old witch awaited him. Gingerly, she scooped him into her arms and smiled down at him.

"Don't ye worry," she told him as she tickled his little button nose. "Ye shall properly be returned to where ye came from."

She carried the boy deep into the woods to where a fire raged in a small clearing. There, she took a sharp blade and cut off his jeweled fingers and toes. Once the valuables were secured, the witch returned the baby to the fire, placing him in the center of the ash. While he burned away, she chanted and danced naked around the fire, giving him back to the element that had given him to the Queen. When nothing was left of the newborn boy, the fire vanished and the smoke cleared.

It had been well over a hundred years since the witch – who had once been known throughout the kingdom as the greatest healer in all the land – had failed to cure an old Queen from what was killing her. The truth was the Queen was not diseased or ill in any way. She had merely been old and it had been her time to go. While the witch could have prolonged her life and allowed her body to continue to deteriorate for countless more years, she had refused. It had seemed like it would be a cruel jest rather than a blessing.

The King had not been so liberal on the view. He saw the witch's refusal as treason. By not saving his beloved Queen, he believed the witch was killing her. When the old Queen eventually died, the King ordered the witch to be burned at the stake. The fire did nothing to her, as it was impossible to burn a witch. He then ordered her to be hung, but when the trapdoor opened beneath her feet for her to drop, she stayed just where she was – hovering in the air as if she was still standing on the trapdoor.

With ancient words that she could not fight, the King's priest cast a spell upon the witch and banished her to the woods outside the kingdom. His spell formed an invisible barrier across the land, impossible for her to penetrate. Her magic was no use against the holy spell, and she'd been forced to recreate her life in the forest.

Now, with the last of the royal bloodline gone, the witch had her revenge. The castle had fallen. Her anger was satisfied. Tomorrow would be a brand new and hopeful day.

This next tale is a wonderful tale to help ye recover from the frightening thoughts of goblins and witches in the forest. It is a tale of youth, beauty and unexpected love. It is the story of a handsome young man who lives in an old and empty castle.

What? That doesn't sound like unexpected love to ya? Well... what if I told ye that it was a dark and stormy night, when all of the sudden came a rapping upon the castle door?

Yes. When I put it like that, it does sound like something magical, doesn't it? Enjoy this endeavor with the Dark Lord of the Castle.

Dark Lord of the Castle

He was the castellan and sole resident of the old Castle Murdrah. A dark lord of great desires, primitive fantasies, and iridescent dreams, Lord Bryce Hansel preferred his solitude within these mighty stone walls. A fortress from the penetrating outside world, this was his sanctuary – a place where he could be alone with his thoughts or, if he wished, he could be in the company of beautiful women... women that he could enjoy for the night and never have to see again.

Handsome, brooding, strong and sleek, Lord Hansel found pleasures when pleasures were needed, and he sought solace when it was required. Currently, he lay in a tub of blood, soaking his naked flesh with its warm and thick deliciousness. It covered him from head to toe and soaked in his hair as he washed away the actions from the bedroom.

He'd had the yearning for the company of a fresh young maiden for the night. He found such a specimen walking along the path, cold and alone. Lord Hansel had offered her a ride in his buggy, which she graciously accepted. He brought her to his castle for a bottle of wine, some light conversation, and some under the sheets mischief. Once they had both been deliciously pleasured, he carried her to the bathroom and placed her in the tub, where he quickly killed her and drained her of her blood. Her body was now in the cellar, where it would rot with the others.

Lord Hansel tasted the maiden's blood and moaned with delight. There was nothing he enjoyed more than basking in nirvana while bathing in the juice of life.

When the bloodbath began to cool, he stood and stepped from the claw-footed tub. With a white towel, he dried himself, cleaning the blood away. The towel was red when he dropped it to the floor. He stepped toward an ornate golden full-length mirror and gazed at his impressive reflection. He looked as young and handsome as ever. This meant the bath worked, as it always did.

Some would have called this ability a curse and some would have considered it a blessing, but bathing in youthful blood kept Lord Hansel young, healthy and attractive. It was a special magic all of his own, and it prevented his true age from ever showing.

Once, he'd bathed in the blood of an elderly woman who he believed he was doing a justice by ending her misery. The bath had resulted in his appearance aging dramatically. It had taken the blood of six beautiful young women to restore his handsome youthfulness.

It had taken the dark lord only once to learn that mistake. That had been many years ago, and it was a mistake he'd vowed to never repeat.

He entered his bed chamber and dressed for the night. Thunder rumbled from the sky outside. Turning his head to the window, Lord Hansel saw lightning illuminate the otherwise dark night sky. Heavy rain began to fall immediately thereafter.

"A storm…" he muttered as he tied to belt to his robe. "Nothing pleases me more."

Leaving his bed chamber behind, he went downstairs to the foyer and turned toward the parlor. There, he sat in a great chair in front of the largest window in the house. It was the perfect place to watch a storm. He'd enjoyed the view from this chair often. A good storm was calming, he believed, and there was nothing better to ready him for sleep.

After taking in the view for a long moment, he stood from his chair and walked across the room to a small bar, where he poured himself a fresh glass of wine. He drank down the first beautiful sip as he returned to his chair. When the glass was around half empty, he heard a rapping upon the front entrance.

At the late hour and especially during such a storm, a visitor of any sort was unexpected. Perhaps, he considered, he'd misheard and it had just been a branch from a tree slapping against something. Then, the heavy knock came again. It was distinctly coming from the entrance.

With his wine in hand, he returned to the foyer and stood before the entrance. The door was heavy and massive and a lesser man would have struggled opening it alone. For Lord Hansel, it was an easy feat.

The door opened wide and on the other side of it stood a

soaking wet but extremely beautiful young woman. She trembled from the cold of the rain.

"Please, sir, might I seek shelter here from the storm?" she begged in a shaky voice. She looked to the dark land behind her and pointed. "My buggy broke a wheel down the road. My horse got loose and ran off. I shall never find him in this storm."

Lord Hansel looked her over and smiled. While he'd just enjoyed the company and blood of an attractive young woman, she'd been nowhere near as beautiful as the one that stood before him. In fact, this girl at his threshold looked absolutely delectable. He stepped aside to let her enter.

"Please, do come in. No one should be outside in such a storm."

He felt flushed with excitement as she entered. He shut the door behind her; it made a large thump that caused the young woman to jump from the startle.

"Thank ye, kind lord," the woman told him when she recovered from the sound of the door closing. "I am afraid the storm has me ready to leap out of my skin."

Lord Hansel considered telling her that he could help her with that. He'd be more than happy to cut the skin away from her body, but he held the urge within.

"I was just enjoying a late-night glass of red wine," he said pleasantly. "Would ye care for some?"

She looked at him and at his glass as if questioning his

offer. Then, after hesitating a moment, she said, "Please. That sounds refreshing."

"Follow me, please."

Lord Hansel led the young woman into his parlor, where she stood before the fire to warm and dry herself. He poured her a glass of red wine and handed it to her. The way her throat clenched as she swallowed enticed him.

There was silence for a moment as he took a seat on a chair near her. He sipped his wine and smiled at her, watching her as she gazed throughout the room.

"Have ye read all of these books?" she asked, taking in the massive collection that filled the many shelves and were stacked near the desk.

"Some," he admitted, "but one day, I hope to have read them all."

"There must be a thousand or more," she continued. "It would take a lifetime to read all of these."

"At least a lifetime," he clarified, "but I don't plan on leaving this world any time soon."

"I thank thee for taking me in," she added and sipped again from the goblet. "The storm came at a most inopportune time."

"Were ye on yer way to someplace important?" He looked at her with a devilish grin. Wet, she was beautiful. He imagined she was even more stunning when dry. He swallowed, thirsting for her.

"No…" she replied, hesitantly. "Well… yes, but not so important now."

Her words were curious to him. What could have been important to her but become less important simply due to breaking a wheel on her buggy? He closed his eyes and nodded, and then sipped again. He decided to be coy with her – to pry without appearing to pry.

"I would be happy to escort thee to wherever ye were heading," he said in a matter-of-fact way. "My buggy is quite spacious and comfortable. We would be shielded from the storm, although my poor horse would surely be drenched." He chuckled at that last part and raised his glass. "To buggies and thunderstorms!" Then, with his cheer, he drank heavily and finished his wine.

"Oh, no, fair lord," the stranger said. He looked at her with a raised eyebrow. "It's… it's much too dangerous in this weather. Should yer horse become spooked, I fear we could both become stranded on the road."

She had chosen her words carefully; Lord Hansel took note of this. It furthered his curiosity over why she was out late at night in a storm and to where she'd been heading.

"M'lady," he told her with an edge in his tone, "I have never been *stranded* anywhere a day in my life."

Lord Hansel stood and refilled his wine. He offered more to his guest, but she'd barely touched what she had. He put the crystal cork back into the bottle and returned to his seat.

"Would ye care for a change of clothes at least?" he asked. There were still his sister's clothes in her old room upstairs. He believed they would be a good fit on this young woman. His dear sister Antonia had been around this stranger's age when she'd met with the end of her time. She had not inherited her brother's ability to heal and rejuvenate the body in a bath of young and healthy blood. Lord Hansel had demonstrated its power to her though, as he had used her blood one night to bathe in.

The woman looked around the room, as if searching for someone else. "Is there somebody else here?" she asked him, looking at him again.

He found the question peculiar. Had she simply assumed he lorded over this castle in solitude, or was it knowledge she somehow already knew? He was finding her more intriguing by the moment.

Once again, he stood and walked to his bookshelves. Running his thumb over several titles, he pulled a tattered old journal and carried it to the oak desk nearby. There, he sat and thumbed through the pages.

"My family has lived within these walls for generations," he told her as he browsed the notes on the pages. "Alas, I am all that remains of my lineage. The clothing I mentioned belonged to my dear sister, long departed from this world."

"Oh," she muttered in what seemed like feigned surprise. "I

am sorry to hear that, m'lord."

"It was a short battle for her," he continued. "She did not suffer for long."

"That sounds like a blessing," the woman noted.

"Death is *always* a blessing." He shut the journal and stood again. At the shelf, he returned it and took one from beside it. Returning to the desk, Lord Hansel asked, "Where did ye say ye were traveling to?"

She looked at him over the rim of the glass as she sipped her wine. "I didn't."

Lord Hansel smiled as he browsed the journal. "Some believe my family was cursed. Many of my bloodline died in most disturbing ways, while others lived healthy and incredibly long lives." Again, he'd chosen the wrong journal from the ones on his shelf. Returning to the shelf, he paid closer attention to the scribbles on their labels and finally found the one he sought. At the desk, he opened it and asked, "Have ye ever danced naked in the rain?"

"Excuse me?"

He glanced at her and saw the surprise from his question. He smiled again. "Forgive the improper question," he said. His finger marked the spot on the page that he'd been seeking. "Good wine has a tendency to make me loose lipped."

"It is forgiven," the woman said and looked away from him, toward the window that he'd earlier looked out. "The rain is heavier now. I do not imagine this storm has any plans on letting up."

"Then ye shall stay the night," Lord Hansel insisted and stood once again. "In my sister's room. The bed is warm and made. There are clothes there for ye to change into. A fireplace to keep the chill out of the room…"

He'd expected the woman to decline the offer, but when she spoke, her response was all too eager. "That would be lovely, m'lord," she told him. Her smile was large. "I shall forever be grateful."

"Follow me," he said and took a lantern to guide their way.

In his dead sister's room, he stoked a fire while the stranger changed clothes behind the dressing screen. As the fire ignited, he looked back toward the screen and even though he could not see her, he could imagine the curves of her delicious flesh as she undressed to change. When she stepped from behind the screen in a white cotton nightgown, he sighed – his moment of fantasy brought to an end.

"It is a good fit," he told her, noting the gown.

She nodded in agreement. "Yes. Thank ye." She stepped toward the mirror and gazed at her reflection. "How did she die?" she asked, touching a hand to the collar of the gown. "Yer sister."

The dark lord stepped up behind her, looking at her reflection with her. "She bled to death, I dare say."

Her eyes grew wide from his response. "I thought ye said it

was quick."

"Aye, it was." His smile broadened and he stepped away from her, toward the dresser nearby. He'd brought with him the journal from the parlor and set it upon the dresser when entering here. Now, he opened it to the page he'd marked earlier.

The thunder sounded with intense threat and rattled the land outside of the castle. Lord Hansel's guest seemed momentarily startled by it, but he didn't mind it one bit.

She laughed at herself after jumping from the thunder. Looking at the dark lord, she noted the journal, asking, "Do ye plan to read to me? Help lull me to sleep?"

"Aye," he acknowledged. "These journals have been in my family for longer than this castle has stood."

"Then ye shall fill my head with thoughts of dragons, knights, and damsels in distress." Her voice was light – nearly giddy. "Perhaps ye shall lay with me as ye read."

"No, m'lady," he said and shrugged. "My reading voice is much better when I stand."

"Then ye shall lay with me after," she insisted. "I frighten terribly in storms. Surely, I will not rest without yer companionship."

Lord Hansel stared at her with a slimmer grin than normal across his face. It was not unusual for women to want to go to bed with him. Nearly every woman that he welcomed into his castle got to experience the distinct flavor of his passionate lovemaking.

To the naked eye, the young woman climbing onto his sister's bed seemed no different than the others. Still, she *was* different; that much he knew for sure.

He locked eyes with her as she settled into a sitting position and relaxed back with her palms supporting her against the mattress. Coyly, she parted her legs, stretching the long dress of the sleeping gown.

"Do not be shy, m'lord," she told him and bit her bottom lip. "I would graciously accept yer... *comfort* in this storm"

She began to undress, unbuttoning the front of the gown so that her pale and perky breasts were exposed. Lord Hansel looked at them and felt a familiar urge grow within him. He shook the urge away, as there was something off-putting about her seductive behavior. It was out of place and uncommon for a woman to act in such a way, especially within a stranger's home.

Even so, he had to play her game. "I simply could not take advantage of a young woman for whom I do not know the name," he said, teasingly.

The woman licked her lips and ran a finger over a perfect rosy nipple. "Esmeralda," she replied and then giggled like a mischievous imp. "My name is Esmeralda."

His eyebrows rose and his ears twitched at the sound of her name. "Esmeralda..." he whispered in a breathy way. "It's a beautiful name, m'lady."

"I am glad ye are fond of it, m'lord." She pulled the hem of the nightgown over her spread knees and gave him a peek of her feminine wonders.

"An old Spanish name, I do believe," Lord Hansel continued. He refused to give into her temptations. She had exposed herself, but not in the way he wished… not yet.

"Do ye not find me desirable?" Esmeralda questioned, pouting through her words. "I can pleasure ye in ways that no other woman would dare."

"I bet ye could," he replied. Outside, the storm made itself known once more as thunder rippled through the sky. "But I believe it is story time." He held the journal up before her and winked.

"If it appeases thee," the woman stated, "then I shall endure yer story, as long as ye agree to endure *me* once it has finished."

Lord Hansel offered his cockiest of grins and made a vow to the lass. "Endurance is the fuel of man."

Intrigued by his reply, Esmeralda growled with anticipation. "Then by all means, m'lord… do tell me a story." Like a young girl at bedtime, she curled up on the bed and watched him with wide, excited eyes.

The dark lord did as requested. He held the journal up before him and began to read aloud words that were so ancient he had no knowledge of their origination. Where required, he said the young woman's name. After the first mention of her, Esmeralda looked away from him and growled again – this time, more venomously. On the second mention, she screamed and her body straightened into a plank, rising above the bed and hovering horizontally with it.

On the third mention, Esmeralda began to twist all about in ways that even the most talented contortionist would have never dared attempt. She screeched and squealed with every twist, snap, and pop of her body. Lord Hansel watched with a grin, continuing to recite the long spell in the journal that had been passed down throughout his family and many others – a spell that would force a creature to reveal its true self.

As he neared the end of the spell, Esmeralda's skin began to change color... it grew brittle and wrinkled. Her hair turned white and stringy, falling out in clumps here and there. Her back became humped, her nose grew large and crooked, and her hands withered – their nails, long and sharp like raven claws.

The spell ended and Esmeralda fell to the bed with a heavy thump. "A glamour!" Lord Hansel exclaimed and closed the book. He set it down and clapped his hands together. A smile filled his face. "Just as I suspected." Heartily, he chuckled.

Esmeralda looked up at him and sneered bitterly. In her true form, she was as old and decrepit as any crone he'd ever known. "How did ye know?" she asked him.

Lord Hansel laughed again. Ending his gleeful laugh with a sigh, he shook his head. "I knew something was off with ye the moment I opened my door," he explained. "It's yer ancient blood. I could smell it – rotten and old. Then, ye tried to seduce me. Had I given in, ye would have snatched my soul right from my body and delivered it to yer Devil."

"And I would be *young* again!" she shouted, raising a weak and trembling fist for emphasis. "And *beautiful*!"

The dark lord still smiled at her, but he did not laugh this time, for he understood her pain. He understood her desire to feel young, beautiful and alive again. It was the same desire that drove him to murder young woman after young woman and bathe in their warm, thick blood. The blood made him become exactly what the old crone wanted to be. How could he possibly fault her on that?

Then, he had the grandest of ideas. His smile widened. The crone's expression became more crazed and worrisome.

"Ye have a glimmer in thy eye," she said in a shaky tone. "What be on yer mind?"

"Perhaps," he said and approached her at the bed, "we can come to some sort of *arrangement*."

The old crone cocked a curious eyebrow. "What kind of *arrangement*?"

Over the next while and by the light of the lantern and the flickering flames that danced in the fireplace, Lord Hansel shared with the crone his secret to eternal youth and beauty. It was decided that the dark lord's victims could serve a double purpose. As Lord Hansel sliced them open to drain them of their blood, Esmeralda would take their souls and deliver them to her Devil.

Thusly, the dark lord moved the old crone into his castle with him and, together, they bathed in the everlasting bliss of eternal youth and impeccable beauty and health. Over time, they grew quite fond of one another, and as they basked in the blood of their beautiful victims, they fell in love and lived happily ever after.

I never said that the path to true love was nice and clean, did I? Heavens no! It's as messy as the blood Lord Hansel bathed in.

True love exists in many different ways. Two lovers who spend their lives together... a mother and her connection with her children... Even siblings often share the bond of true love. When a true love is taken, one shall stop at nothing to get it back. It is the way of nature.

Thusly, when a boy's sister is taken away to a place forbidden for travel, he will take a most horrific path to save her, even if it costs him his life. Many dangers await ye within this story, dear reader. I hope yer ready for The Woman with Wings.

The Woman with Wings

Once upon a summer afternoon, a brother and sister went frolicking in the woods, in search of berries and wildflowers. Their parents were long dead, and so it was up to them to scavenge for their food every day. They enjoyed making games of it, like chasing one another through the winding forest paths or even pelting each other with berries that were rotten on the stems.

It was raining on this particular afternoon, and the siblings became wet and muddy as they played and hunted their food and foliage.

"Sister," the brother called in warning as she glided swiftly across the slick mud, "ye shouldn't run so fast near there! That hill be steep!"

"Bah!" she squealed, giggled, and spun around in a circle. "It's lovely to slip and slide! Join me!" She squealed again and spun once more. Then, she lost her footing and tumbled backward. Brother watched as she fell off the ledge, tumbling down the hill.

"Sister!" he shouted and then slipped and slid his way to her in a hurried but cautious manner. "Sister, are ye alright?"

Brother looked over the ledge, staring down as he watched his sister roll to the foot of the hill. He began after her but came to a pause as a winged creature swooped down from the sky and gathered Sister into its grip. In the blink of an eye, the creature swooped upward again with Sister in tow.

"Sister!" he cried out again and watched as the creature carried his sister to the great forbidden mountain, which was a good day's trek away by foot.

Distraught, the brother contemplated how to save his twin sister. He knew he would have to venture to the forbidden mountain and climb its dangerous terrain. Once he found his sister, he would also find the creature that had taken her. Surely, a battle would ensue. Before going after his sister, he had to be well prepared.

Brother swiftly returned to the small home in the woods and retrieved his bow and satchel of arrows, as well as his hunting knife. He also gathered a grappler and some rope in case he needed it on the mountain's more challenging regions.

He was hungry, but he hadn't the time to think about food. Thusly, he ignored the few berries and nuts he and his sister had gathered, and he set off down the steep hill in which Sister had tumbled.

At the bottom, he found her shoe and took it, tucking it into the bag he carried over his shoulders. Surely, Sister would need it when they made their escape from the mountain.

There were three distinct paths that cut through the woods on this side of the hill. One led to the forbidden mountain, one to a swamp said to be the habitat of goblins and trolls, and one path led to the sea. He knew it was the path to his left that led to the sea, as that was the direction the streams winded toward. Of the other two paths, he was unsure. Both were incredibly dangerous, and neither had he ever ventured through before. He'd only heard the rumors and the tales of horror from those who'd walked them and survived.

It was through one of these paths that the twins' parents met their demise. They had been eaten by a monstrous troll – all but their heads. Their heads were returned to the twins' home and left on the doorstep for them to discover.

That had been when the twins were little, and they'd stayed clear of this side of the hill and its treacherous paths ever since.

Now, Brother had no choice but to travel through one, and seeing that the mountain appeared straight ahead of him – far away but towering high above the peaks of the trees – he decided to take the center path. It was the most obvious one to him, and with a murmuring of self-encouragement, he set forth to find his sister.

It was dark down this path. The trees all seemed to fold toward one another high above, blocking out much of the sunlight. There were sounds down this path that he'd never heard elsewhere in the woods, and they made him tremble with anxious fear as he walked.

The further he ventured, the more foul the air became. It smelled of rot and death. Brother fought away the urge to be sick, but the temptation managed to linger as the scent grew stronger.

He heard the sound of slowly moving water, which meant

there was a stream up ahead. Brother felt like he was off his course – like he'd chosen the wrong path – and he hoped the stream might help guide him in the right direction. If the stream flowed in a direction horizontal to that which he walked, he could walk against its flow and follow its banks to the correct path.

After a bit of time and walking had passed, Brother came to the stream and a bridge that offered crossing to the other side of the path. The terrible scent was the strongest here, and Brother felt the urge to be sick rise up and threaten him once more.

He looked at the water and tumbled back, away from it. It barely moved and was red with blood. Hundreds of skeletal parts and decaying bodies filled it to where almost no water could be seen at all. He gasped and covered his nose and mouth with his sleeve.

Brother stood from the ground and collected himself, though not once moving his eyes from the terror in the stream. Then, once he couldn't look at it any longer, he looked to the bridge. Walking along the banks of this stream was something he was not willing to do, and so he had to press forward. Wrong path or not, this direction *would* take him to the mountain if he simply walked straight ahead.

He stepped onto the bridge, only to be pushed back by a sudden rumbling as a large creature leapt to the middle of it. A troll, Brother realized. He felt his heart thump against his chest so fast that he wondered if he'd die from it.

He had, indeed, chosen the wrong path. With one hand grasping the handle of his hunting knife, he prepared for a battle.

The grim troll took a few steps toward him and came to a stop. It stood tall and mighty, towering over young Brother. It was smiling at him. Awkward fangs lifted up over the top lip and curled down the bottom one. They were covered in slimy drool.

"Ye has trespassed on me land," the troll told him in a booming voice that made his head throb. "Ye shall now be my supper."

Brother swallowed through a knot in his throat and tried to compose himself in a way that his fear would not show… if that was at all possible. "I mean thee no harm," he told the giant troll. "I just wish to cross this bridge on my route to the forbidden mountain."

The troll looked at him for a moment and then laughed a heavy, bellowing chuckle. "Ye have chosen the wrong path, boy!" he exclaimed once his laughter subsided.

"Will this path not lead me to the mountain as well?" Brother questioned.

"Aye," said the troll, "but only those who answer my riddle may pass this bridge and continue. All others meet their fate and become a part of my red stream of death." It gestured to the bloody, cluttered stream around them. "Few have ever been successful, and those who have still likely perished in the woods beyond this point."

Brother had a feeling that even if he declined the riddle and offered to leave this path the way he came, the troll would not let him. He had no choice but to accept the beast's offer and chance answering the riddle. If he failed, he would fight.

"I accept yer challenge," Brother said, knowing it was his only real option. "What is yer riddle, troll?"

The troll looked him over again and then stepped back to the center of the bridge. In a lower tone than before, it recited its challenge. "I be something people love or hate. I change their appearances and thoughts. For those who take care, I shall go up. For others, I shall fool them. For some, I be a mystery. Some may try to hide me, but I will always show my true self. No matter how hard people try, I shall *never* go down." Grimly, he asked, "What am I?"

Brother smirked at the puzzle's delivery. It seemed so obvious that the answer was *time*, and he opened his mouth to blurt the word out. Yet, just before it could leave his lips, he stalled. That seemed too easy. How many of those poor lost souls in the stream of blood had blurted out that very word, thinking they were right? It had to be something else – something that was similar, but not the trick of the word *time*.

He thought it over for a moment, keeping his eyes averted from the troll and the stream. The troll stood still with a smile watching him. It seemed to have all the patience in the world while Brother took his time.

The puzzle was challenging and he was young with limited life experience. For the first time in a long time, he wished he was older and wiser and could process this riddle more maturely. As he considered this, a thought came to him and his smile grew to match the troll's.

"Age," he said in a voice as certain as the sunrise in the mornings. "Ye be age." He took a step forward toward the beastly creature. "Age always shows and never goes down in number. Many try to hide their age, and everyone changes with it."

The troll looked at him strangely. Then, it growled something low but fierce. Folding its arms before it, the creature stood its ground.

"I answered yer riddle," Brother told the troll and took another step near it. "Now, ye shall let me pass."

The troll laughed at him. "Aye, ye answered my riddle, correctly at that. Now, ye must pay the toll."

"Payment?" Brother asked, baffled. "Ye said nothing of payment before."

"Ye must pay the price, or else ye shall be eaten," the troll threatened.

"And what be it that ye desire?"

"A kidney," the troll announced. "Ye have two. Ye only need one to survive."

The price seemed extreme, but if he didn't pay it, Brother knew he was doomed, and his sister would be doomed along with him. Painstakingly, he took off his backpack and removed his shirt. Then, with his hunting knife, he stared at the troll and held back his screams and tears as he cut out his own kidney. Once it was removed, he tossed it to the troll's feet.

Brother used his shirt to pack and secure his fresh wound. He wouldn't be able to properly stitch it until he returned home. He felt immense pain, but he kept it within as best he could as he watched the troll pick up his kidney. The troll sniffed it and, after a brief inspection, popped it into its mouth in one big bite. Brother stared in horror as the creature chomped up his kidney and swallowed it down, moaning in satisfaction.

"Ahh…" the troll murmured and licked its lips. "Ye be the first brave lad to have ever answered the riddle *and* paid the toll. Ye may pass." Leaping from the bridge, the troll disappeared as suddenly as it had appeared.

Even in as dire pain as he was, Brother gathered his things and hurried across the bridge to the other side, refusing to glance again at the stream of death – no matter how tempted he was to do so. Once on the other side with the bridge to his back, he exhaled a heavy sigh of relief.

He was weak and woozy as he ambled down the path and through the thick woods. Brother felt the wetness of his blood as the fresh wound steadily bled out. Soon, he was able to go no further. His world began to spin and everything went dark.

When he awoke, he was inside of a small dwelling atop a

wooden table. Weakly, he looked to his wound. There was a fresh bandage over it and no blood could be seen.

Everything was cloudy at first, but his vision cleared and he sat upright, wincing from the pain.

"Ye should rest," he heard a woman's voice say from nearby. "Ye don't want to pop yer stitches."

"Where am I?" he asked as he lay back flat against the table.

"Ye be in my little cabin, safe and sound," the woman told him in an assuring tone. "I see ye paid the bridge toll. We don't ever see yer kind in this neck of the woods."

"My kind?" he questioned. "What kind is that?"

"Mortal," she said and snickered. "The troll always has a feast with yer kind."

Brother trembled. He lifted up enough to look for the woman. He saw her nearby, sitting atop a wicker chair. She was old and lovely. Slender and stunning with long white hair that fell down in heavy locks around her black robe. There were some age lines on her face, but her smile was impeccable. Her eyes, dark and entrancing.

"Who are ye?" he asked her, although he was leary of the answer.

"I am Anastasia," she said in a silky-smooth tone. "Witch of the Enchanted Woods. Tell me, mortal. What gave ye the courage to travel this far? Why has thee come all this way?"

Brother swallowed. He was incredibly thirsty. "My sister," he began, hunting for the words, "was captured by a mighty winged creature and taken to the forbidden mountain." He swallowed again. His throat hurt from it. "I – I must rescue her."

"That is a challenge I am afraid ye cannot handle physically," she told him. Even though he knew she was right, he didn't want to hear it. "However, I can *restore* yer health *and* ensure ye safely reach the edge of the forbidden mountain." She stood and stepped from her chair, walking to him. Looking over him, she added, "I can even ensure a safe passage home for yer sister and thee."

It sounded remarkable and too good to be true. Still, he graciously thanked her. "That would be wonderful! I would forever be indebted to thee."

"No," she said, shaking her head. "No, ye won't, for this magic comes with a price."

Of course, he thought and groaned. "What be yer price, witch?"

The old witch smiled more broadly and said, "The head of the winged creature that hath taken yer sister."

It was a strange request, Brother thought, but he considered it. He would likely have to slay the beast anyway when saving his sister. What would it matter if he took the head afterward? Surely, it was more than a fair trade for his and his sister's safety.

"Fine then," he told her. "Heal me and provide the safety

for my sister and me that ye say ye will, and ye shall have the head of the winged creature upon my return."

The old witch clapped her hands together and cackled loudly. Then, hovering over him with her face near his and her hand over his wound, she began to chant. He felt a sharp, sudden pain, but as her chanting ended, so did the pain. She stepped back and Brother sat upright, feeling better than he'd felt in his entire life. He touched his hand to his wound. It felt as if the kidney had never been removed.

"Return to me with the head and I shall keep my word, ensuring a safe journey," she said eagerly. "Fail to bring me the head, and ye shall never make it home alive."

"Wait! What?" Brother questioned, but as he spoke the words and the witch clapped her hands together, he found he was transported outside of her small dwelling – back on the path toward the forbidden mountain.

On his journey through the remainder of the woods, Brother found himself well protected, just as the witch had vowed. He was neither attacked nor approached by any woodland predator. Not once did he lose his footing or even his way. His endurance stayed high, and he grew neither thirsty nor hungry. Yet, once he reached the foot of the forbidden mountain, the witch's enchantment of safety ended. His endurance dropped and he became hungry and thirsty once again. He was tired, and looking up at the impending mountain, his climb looked impossible.

Somewhere on that mountain was his sister, however, and that was all of the encouragement he needed to push him forward. Using his grappler and rope, along with his drive and determination, he began to scale the mountain with little incident. About halfway up, he looked below and saw the tops of the trees staring up at him. The sight made him a bit dizzy and he had to close his eyes for a moment to prevent blacking out.

Brother took a few calming breaths, tilted his head upward, and opened his eyes. With his world no longer spinning, he resumed the treacherous climb.

Twice, he lost his footing and nearly fell to his death. On one of those occasions, the rock beneath his foot had crumbled away from his weight, causing him to lose his balance. On the other occasion, he overturned a stone stepping up onto it. Both times, his grappler had been his saving grace.

Finally, after many hours and an exhausting climb, he reached a flat area near the very top of the forbidden mountain. It took some effort for him to pull himself over onto the ground. He was weak from the venture, hungry and thirsty. When he was finally on firm ground, he noticed it was grassy, flowering, and beautiful.

Brother stood up straight and surveyed his surroundings. He stood at the foot of a lovely meadow with a glorious palace located at the far edge of it. He knew beyond a shadow of a doubt that this was where the winged creature had brought his beloved sister.

He looked at the smallish but beautiful palace ahead of him and the golden cobblestone path that led to it. On either side of the path were magnificent trees that bore fruits that Brother had never seen before. Each was colorful and looked scrumptious.

The front and main structure of the palace was rounded at the top like a dome, with large windows and an entrance that looked like it was built for a queen. Several columns lined the lower portion of the palace, staggering off from side to side to build an arched, half-circle porch.

On either side of the dome structure were two towers. At the top of each was a giant bird cage. Brother could barely see them from where he stood, but he noticed a distinct difference between the two cages. One of them was occupied. He was certain the occupant was his sister.

Up the golden cobblestone path, Brother began to run. The palace drew closer to him, and he kept his eyes upward at the cage. Even though its perception changed as he neared the palace, he could see more clearly that it was, indeed, a young woman within the cage, and he was more confident than before that the woman was Sister – awaiting rescue.

As he approached the large ornate door with golden trim, Brother came to a stop. Suddenly, despite having his bow and arrows and his hunting knife with him, he felt rather helpless. What if this winged beast was mightier than he? The enchanted woods were filled with brilliant, mystical creatures that had abilities far beyond his, and the mountain surely wasn't called forbidden purely because of the treacherous climb up it.

He had no plan aside from rushing through this entrance and storming his way up to the nest in the west tower. Surely, that wouldn't be good enough. Not to mention, once he did rescue his sister, he still had to claim the head of the winged creature.

Brother knew he had to be brave and do what was needed if he and Sister wished to leave this mountain and the Enchanted Woods with their lives. He mustered up what strength he could and pushed on the large door before him. It opened easily, revealing a stunning and grand entranceway. At the center of the entranceway positioned before the back wall was a golden perch that was large enough to fit a man. On either side of it were winding stairs going to another floor. To Brother's left and right were the halls for the West and East wings of the palace.

With no one in sight to stop him, he turned toward the West Wing and started down the hall.

"Intruder!" he heard a woman's voice announce. There was a deep tone of warning in it.

Brother froze in his steps. Nervously, he turned slowly around. There, at the center of the entrance foyer where he'd just stood was the winged creature. Yet, she was not nearly as terrifying in appearance as he'd believed. Her wings and the feathers that covered her head and body were the colors of an ever-changing prism, igniting spectrums of flickering rainbows across nearly every inch of her. Her face, the shape of her body, the tone of her voice… those were all very distinctly that of a woman.

The winged woman took a step nearer him. "Why hath thou trespassed into my home… my kingdom? This mountain is my domain, and mine alone."

"I have come for my sister," he told her in as firm a tone as he could manage. "Ye have taken her and trapped her in a cage atop a tower." He was angry as he spoke, but he was also still very much intimidated by this mystical woman with wings before him.

"Thy sister is my prisoner," she told him, smiling. "I shall dine on her this very evening."

Brother couldn't believe his ears. How could a woman like this creature in front of him wish to feast on a creature so similar in creation? It sickened the young lad, and he no longer cared that he had to retrieve the winged woman's head. He was all too eager to kill her.

He started to pull his bow and an arrow from his bag when he opted for the hunting knife at his side instead. Gripping it firmly, he charged toward her, ready to slay.

When he was just more than an arm's length from her – hunting knife's tip included – the woman with wings opened her mouth so wide that it stretched to nearly double in length the size of her head. She released a sound so amplified that it came at him with the force of a typhoon, throwing him off his feet and sending him flying backward. He landed with a hard thump at the far end of the hallway.

The sound emitted from the winged woman made his head ache and his nose and ears bleed. He cringed with his eyes clamped shut, plugging his ears until the sound ended. When the bird woman silenced, he looked at her in terror.

"Ye shall join thy sister, but caged in the East tower," she told him in a voice as normal as that of any mortal woman. "There, ye shall bake beneath the sun until I am ready to devour thee."

She said it so matter-of-factly, and that was perhaps the most terrifying thing about it. Sure, he didn't want to be eaten, and he didn't want his sister to be eaten either. But it was the way she *said* it, as if it was no big deal to her… something she'd done a million times before.

And perhaps she had…

While Brother was grounded, he tried to grab his bow and an arrow in an attempt to defend himself, but his hands were much too shaky. His grip was weak from fear.

"It shall do thee no good to fight," the bird-like creature told him as she approached. "Come with me willingly, and ye shall experience a quick and merciful end.

When she reached him, he surrendered his bow and arrow to the floor. With his hands free once again, he gripped his hunting knife from beside him and stood. The woman with wings noticed the knife immediately. A much more powerful explosion of sound than before flooded out of her enormous mouth and instantly turned Brother to stone.

She placed him in the meadow near a beautiful tree, where he would serve as a sort of scarecrow to frighten away the crows from the fruit. Then, as painstakingly slowly as she could, she feasted on Sister, who screamed in agony with every chomp the bird woman took.

I imagine by now ye be ready for something nice and fluffy. Am I right? Well, too bad, dearie. If anything, this next story is anything but nice or fluffy.

Perhaps, the story can be considered justified, depending on yer way of looking at naughty children and their punishments. When every other punishment fails on a bad little boy or girl, there is one option left. Make 'em eat dirt!

The results will astound ya. It certainly does the little boy in this next story, whose parents simply cannot take anymore of the lad's torture. This is When the Children Eat the Dirt.

When the Children Eat the Dirt

There once was a place where children went when they left this life too soon. Their bodies were carried to a special clearing in an enchanted forest. A small box-shaped hole was dug several feet deep and the deceased child was quartered and placed within it. The pieces of the body were stacked, with the legs folded at the bottom, then the torso, followed by the arms. The head was placed on top, always looking up to the sky with its eyes and mouth open. This was to ensure the dirt entered the mouth when the hole was filled.

If the burial was done right, a heavy rain would fall throughout the next day and night. Three days following, the small beginnings of a new Life Tree would push up from the ground. These Life Trees were considered the rarest and most stunning of all trees in the enchanted forest. They lived longer than any other trees in the world, and they carried with them the souls and energies of the dead children, letting them live again within the roots, branches, leaves and fruits.

For a dead child, it was the most honorable burial possible. For a living child, the results were very much different.

"I don't want to go!" young Brennan screeched as his parents dragged him by his wrists across the meadow. The meadow was filled with so many Life Trees that the scent of their flowering blossoms was overwhelming. There was also much fresh ground left, ready to fertilize the remains of dead boys and girls. This was not where Brennan wanted to be, nor was it where he belonged. "Ye cannot make me!"

"Aye, but we can!" Father told him with a sinister smile and a chuckle to match it. "And we shall!"

"Ye have been an incredibly naughty little boy," Mother added in a matter-of-fact way. "Ye haven't obeyed us... well... *ever*, and this place is made for bad children like ye."

"I won't do it!" he protested loudly, fighting to break free of his parents' firm grips. Kicking and screaming, he gave it all he had, but he simply wasn't strong enough. "I won't let ye bury me!"

"Ah, like ye could stop us!" Father said and laughed again. "We warned ye what would happen if ye continued to be disobedient. Now, ye shall experience it firsthand."

Brennan cried and screamed and begged and cursed as he was dragged through the meadow to a spot that had a shovel sticking up from the ground. Father had with him a bag that he dropped to his feet. Within it, he took some rope and bound Brennan's hands and feet while Mother held the boy steady.

They left his mouth open and unobstructed. After all, he had to eat the dirt for the ritual to work.

Brennan's wails and pleas continued while Father dug the deep, square hole. It was a challenge for him to get the shape right, as he'd had to climb down into it and dig in the small confined space in order for it to be deep enough. Once he was in to his chin, he decided it was just right and, with Mother's help, climbed out.

"Ye should have listened to us," Mother told her child as she pinched his tearstained cheeks. Her smile was as maniacal as her wide, green eyes. "Ye should have behaved. Now… ye must eat the dirt."

Mother blindfolded Brennan so that he could not see. Then, with Father's help, they lifted the boy and lowered him down into the hole and onto his feet. He crouched low to the ground and looked upward, steadily begging for his release. As he cried out, he felt a shovel's worth of dirt slap down against his face and fall into his mouth. He tried to spit it out, but it was no use. The dirt kept coming – so much so that he was forced to swallow it down in order to breathe. Finally, there was so much dirt that it became impossible for him to swallow it all, and even more impossible for him to breathe.

He could no longer hear his parents, only his own thoughts as they ravaged his mind with worries and horror. Without the ability to breathe in or exhale out, he grew dizzy and faint. Eventually, he passed out in his grave. Then, from deep beneath him, tentacle-like roots rose up to him and wrapped themselves around his limbs and torso. They worked their ways into his ears, up his nose, and down his throat. Within a moment's time, he was locked inside a cocoon of roots and dirt, ready for the second stage of the ritual to begin.

Unlike with the children who were quartered and buried dead, it did not rain over Brennan's grave. Instead, Mother watered his grave several times throughout the next day, including a special herbal ingredient in the water that was taken from a special mushroom just beyond the meadow's edge.

The watering, along with the special ingredient, made the roots around and inside of Brennan glow a bright blue. They filled him with an ancient magic that began a transformation lasting throughout the next two days.

During this transformative period, worms began to crawl inside of the root cocoon, attracted by the beauty of the mushroom glow and the stench of the child's flesh. Although he was somehow still alive, his body began to shed its skin like a bird molts feathers or a snake, its skin. Brennan remained unconscious through all of this, and so he had no way of knowing when the worms crawled into his body and began to feed and multiply.

His old insides were of little use to him now, anyway. The worms could feast on them all they wanted; it made no difference. Little Brennan was changing – evolving... morphing into something completely different from the terrible child he'd once been. He'd tormented small woodland creatures... burned trees for the sake of seeing them burn. He'd dissected his little sister Whipples, and he'd drank the blood of their only horse, thinking that it would make him big and strong like the beast had been. Brennan had destroyed anything of value within his family's farm, and he'd more than once put his parents in harm's way. Once, he cut off his mother's hair with a carving knife while she slept. On another occasion, he bit off his father's earlobe, chewing it up and spitting it out – all because he'd been threatened with punishment for some other naughty deed.

A liar, a tormenter, and a bully, Brennan was entered into his punishment by parents who'd found no other option for him. At least, in the spectacular meadow with its ancient and magical properties, he would still have life. He'd driven them insane enough that he was fortunate they hadn't killed him flat out, although some would have considered a quick death more of a blessing than what was happening to him now.

While the worms fed, a new beginning grew within the boy. It pushed out through the shell of his body and the cocoon of roots that held it safe. Without this cage of safety, he lost his form and his sense of what he truly was.

From above, Mother watered his plot again, and as the water made its way to him, Brennan felt himself take on a new shape. In this new form, he was able to push upward and squirm between the moist and loosened soil. He felt parts of him stretch and cling to patches of soil as he shot up past them, and when he poked up above the ground, found he was rooted in place.

"There he be," Mother said, her voice booming as she towered high above him. "There's my boy."

Brennan wanted to call out to her, but he couldn't make a

sound. It occurred to him then that he had no mouth from which to speak with. He did have eyes, and he saw her massive hand come toward him with a gardening spade.

Helpless to defend himself, he braced his arms – thin like stems – and closed his eyes. The ground around him shook and crumbled as Mother loosened it around him. Then, Brennan was uprooted and dumped into a terracotta pot, filled with soil.

"Stay still for Mother," she insisted as she worked his roots into the soil and then filled in any bare spots. "Are ye thirsty? Have a drink." She lifted the watering can and soaked him, the soil, and his roots. "Atsa good boy, now."

He felt the pull as he was lifted by his pot off the ground and then swiftly carried from the meadow and down the long and winding path that led to the family farm. All the while, Mother talked to him about this and that – practically anything that she could think of, as she explained talking help plants grow big and strong. If anything, the constant sound of his mother's bellowing voice as she rambled on about stuff he cared nothing about was enough to drive him insane. He wanted to scream at her and tell her to shut up, but he couldn't say a word or do anything in protest.

When they finally reached the farmhouse, Brennan was brought inside and set atop the round wooden table beneath the front window.

"There ye be," Mother said as she admired him. "Yer sure to get plenty o' light there."

"How long 'til he's ready?" he heard his father ask from somewhere nearby.

"A few weeks," Mother replied in a gingerly way. "A month at best."

"Finally, the little imp will be worth his weight around here." Father chuckled and Brennan's tiny stemmed branches trembled.

Over the next few weeks, Brennan became used to his new position in life. His mother dusted his branches and watered him every day, and several times a week, she put him atop the windowsill or even brought him outside for fresh air and to make the most out of the sunlight. It was a much simpler life than he'd experienced before, and all of the angst, anger and anxiety that had once plagued him were gone and forgotten… things in the past.

Father had become more attentive to him also. He would come over several times a day and check the weight of his branches. While Brennan had two tiny eyes at the center of his stalk, he couldn't turn in either direction to see exactly what sort of fruit or flower he was growing, but he was certain it was heavy and magnificent. Father giggled giddy with delight every time he noticed the growth, and Brennan believed he was beginning to care for him like a son again, instead of looking at him like the atrocity of a person he used to be. Even though he'd been rebirthed and grown into some sort of plant, he had a happy family and that was something that filled him with glee.

A few days later, his little branches grew so incredibly heavy that they began to drag. Finally, as some drooped toward the front of him, he could see his foliage. He instantly became a bit leery and frightened. His stems and their leaves didn't look like stems and leaves at all. Neither did the large rounded welts that formed all over them. Out of the several branches on his thin and young body, Brennan could only see a few, but he could feel by the weight of the others that they were just the same – grotesquely unusual and heavily laden.

He thought, in fact, that his branches and stems and whatever grew on them looked an awful lot like flesh – peachy-white and clean of hair. But such a thing was impossible. Brennan was a plant, and plants had no flesh.

Something felt very wrong now. He heard his mother exclaim as she approached him. "Oh, it's time!" she bellowed blissfully. "Father, bring the platter!"

Brennan wondered what platter she intended.

"And the knife!" Mother added. Brennan screamed deep within himself.

He heard Father as he hurried into the room. In Father's hands were a large serving platter and a big carving knife.

"Finally!" Father explained as he checked out his son's branches. "He wasn't worth much as a boy, but he's finally worth something as a Meat Plant!"

A Meat Plant...? What is a Meat Plant, Brennan wondered.

Mother took the knife from Father and gripped it in one hand while the other chose a branch with plump swelling. She looked into her son's beady plant eyes and told him, "This may hurt just a wee bit, Lad."

Then, quite savagely, she began to slice off the meat that was growing from his branches. Brennan wanted to scream, to cry out, to plea for her to stop. He saw his blood-like juices spray about with every cut she made.

"Oh, he's a juicy one!" Father said with a gleeful chuckle as mother sliced off another plump portion and placed it on the tray.

"I think that be enough for one day," she said and handed Father the knife. "But, oh… how wonderful this is!"

"Aye!" Father agreed and turned away to carry the tray into the kitchen. "And just think of it, Mother! Brennan should produce enough meat to keep us in good supply for many years to come!"

"We have to trim him at least once every other day," Mother agreed, "or else the meat will get tough."

Every other day… years to come… Brennan's blissful reconnection with his family had taken a horrific turn that he had not expected. He was no longer their son to any degree. He was now a source of food for his parents, and for the remainder of his days, he was doomed to be carved and feasted from.

Dear reader, have ye ever felt so lonely that yer only true companionship seems to come from nature? Aye, the feeling is known far and wide. Some fill that void of companionship with their work or crafts. Others pass the time by simply being.

There are also those who might not seem so lonely – the ones popular amongst the people because of a certain skill that they can offer. Such is the story of a carpenter named Jacob, who longs for friendship in a village that sees him only as his work. There are great enchantments in the magical forest, and perhaps he will find more companionship than he bargains for. Enjoy Jacob and the People Tree.

Jacob and the People Tree

Out on a walk one sunny afternoon was a lonely young man named Jacob, who longed for companionship and friends. He busied himself with his carpentry work and spent most of his free time outdoors and wandering about in nature. Whenever he felt down, a beautiful day always helped to cheer him up.

Jacob wasn't completely without the company of other people. As a prominent carpenter with a reputation that spread throughout the kingdom, he was kept busy with customers wishing for him to build this style chair or that type of table for them. He had a gift for woodworking that others couldn't compete with, but his gift seldom brought general conversation. Only more work orders and more demand for his services.

This was a reason he was thankful for nature. On his walks, he got to be free from his trade and was able to casually let the time pass. If he took his breaks to wander through the village or visit with neighbors, there was no rest from his work. It seemed to be the only conversation anyone could think of when visiting with him.

When he needed someone to talk to – someone who wouldn't ask him how work was or wonder if he would have the time to build some meticulously outrageous piece of furniture for them – he would converse with the trees, plants, and woodland animals around him. Some would likely have thought him mad for such behavior, but it seemed to be the only thing that helped keep Jacob sane.

Currently, he walked down a wonderfully smooth dirt pathway that was lined with wildflowers that grew on either side. The forest was sparse here, with trees only every few feet. This gave plenty of room for sunlight to bring flowers, shrubbery, and bright green grass to the landscape.

The further he traveled, the thicker the forest began to grow. There was a stream nearby, and quite often on these walks, Jacob was blessed with seeing wildlife drink from it. On this day, he saw a young deer, lapping away at the fresh flowing water while its parents stood guard nearby. The sight made Jacob smile, and it was one of many reasons he enjoyed walking this particular path more than the others he frequented.

Jacob let the young deer be and he whistled as he continued his walk. He'd set out early this afternoon, and as he'd decided to take the rest of the day off away from his laboring work, he was in no rush to return home. Up ahead was a large round stone where he always rested, relaxed, and enjoyed the sunshine and scenic view. It was also marked the end of his venture down the path, as he would always return home after his rest.

Today, for the first time, he decided to bypass that lovely and relaxing stone. He wasn't by any means tired or ready to relax or nap. He felt energized and chipper, and he was surrounded by his woodland friends… his *only* friends, but friends who welcomed him into their domain with seemingly open arms.

"Oiko, doiko, ba dunk dunk dunk," he sang cheerfully to himself as he strolled down the path – a path that grew narrower the further he walked. "Watch out for the stinky skunk!" It was a silly song he sang – one he'd made up long ago on a walk such as this, where he'd encountered a skunk that fortunately *hadn't* stunk.

As the path grew narrower and the forest thicker, everything became darker – shrouded in shadows. Several of the flowers and plants nearby glowed when shadowed, and they helped to make the scenery more mystical and brighter. Never before had he seen such glowing plants as these. They were remarkable and glowed softly in a vast array of color. He knelt down to one such flower and sniffed it, wondering if it smelled as marvelous as it looked. It was, indeed, the sweetest scent he'd inhaled in perhaps forever.

He stood and sighed. It felt like he'd found a sort of nirvana – a land of beauty and wonder. It was so magical that he yearned to bring a part of its splendor home with him. Crouching down once more, he leaned to the flower he'd sniffed and started to pluck it.

"I wouldn't do that if I were ye," he heard a voice say. It startled him, and Jacob unhanded the flower and stood upright.

Turning around, he looked for the voice's source but saw no one. Deciding it had been nothing more than his imagination playing some tomfoolery on him, he shrugged it off and turned back to the flower.

"Ye should never pick anything from here," the voice spoke again, and once more, Jacob turned around to see its speaker.

Again, there was nobody.

"Perhaps I *am* going mad," he contemplated aloud and then chuckled. "Ah well... being so lonely can do that to a man, I imagine."

"Mad!" another voice noted, mimicking what Jacob had said. Whilst the first voice had sounded male, this one sounded like the voice of an old woman. "Ye will know mad if ye pick one flower from this path!"

"Who said that?" Jacob asked, looking all around. Still, he saw no one. For a moment, he considered he was hearing the voices of ghosts, but if a ghost was going to speak, surely it would have shown itself. "Where are ye?"

Everything was quiet again as he sought for the mysterious voices. He looked all around and even down low, but he could find nobody. When he was about to give up in his search and leave this place behind, he heard giggling from above.

High above him from within the many branches of the tree nearest him, Jacob saw tiny naked people hanging from stems. Men and women alike dangled like fruit, as if just waiting to be plucked.

"Eek!" he screamed and took a heavy step back. Never

before had he seen such a sight. A tree that grew... *people*? How was such a thing even possible? Jacob knew very well where people came from, and neither this nor a cabbage patch was correct. "What... what *are* ye?"

He knew very well what they were; they were tiny people hanging from stems. What he didn't understand was how they were so small, and how they had presumably grown from this tree.

"I be a man!" one shouted. Jacob spotted him deep in the leaves. He had a long white beard and was balding on top. "What do I look like? A mongoose?"

"I be a man too!" shouted another. "And I be a woman!" called a third. Soon, so many tiny voices were bellowing out their genders, as if Jacob was too ignorant to be able to tell who was a man and who was a woman.

"Yer *people*!" he told them in a statement that was close to being a question. "Growing from a tree!" He laughed – a light *hah* – and shook his head. "Perhaps I laid down on that big stone after all and drifted to sleep. This simply *must* be a dream."

"Why ye sound so surprised?" the little balding old man asked. He huffed and folded his tiny arms. "Look at ya – the size of a giant! Ye must have grown from one fertile bunch o' weeds to have gotten so big."

"Big?" Jacob scoffed. "Why, I'm the size of any average man!" After saying this, he realized to the people on the tree that he was likely an enormous, overwhelmingly large man. It amazed him that they weren't frightened of him. At least, he didn't believe they were. "So, how did ye get up in that tree? Somebody's idea of a cruel joke? Are ye sewn to those branches or have ye been nailed into them?" He didn't see any sign of stitching or any nails – only the stems from which each hung.

"How painful!" one of the tiny women gasped. Others then gasped with her. "Oh, heavens no!"

"We bloomed here just like anyone born of a People Tree," the old balding one injected. "This be our home, from our first budding to the time we fall from our branches."

"Fascinating," Jacob said, and on his tiptoes, he inched upward for a closer look at the creatures. A few of them tried to scramble back from him, but their motions merely made them sway on their stems.

"Phew!" one of the tiny people said as she waved a hand in front of her face. "Please, could ye not breathe so closely?"

Jacob chuckled at the comment. His heavy breath made the tiny people sway again. "My apologies," he told them and then lowered down to his regular height. Taking a step back, he added, "I've never seen people such as thee, nor have I heard of a People Tree."

"The large man be unenlightened," the old balding person announced.

"Unintelligible!" shouted another.

"Now, let us not be crude," said a third. "The young man

~ 160 ~

may just be unworldly. How many giants have we seen in our days?"

The large grouping of tiny people muttered amongst themselves for a moment. Jacob found their banter highly entertaining, if a bit insulting.

"I've seen four in my time," the old balding one told the crowd. Everyone hushed around him. "I've been here longer than anyone, and I can promise, the giants are not to be handled lightly!"

"Excuse me, but as the giant in question," Jacob began, seeking clarification, "what dost thou mean by *handled lightly?*"

The little old man laughed bitterly at him. Every tiny eye on the tree watched and waited. "I have seen it with me own eyes enough to know what yer kind is really like," he said. "Two of the giants ran from here in terror when they gazed upon us in our tree. The other two – they were different. They were curious about us, and they insisted we were some sort of fruit. They each picked one of us, and then – right before our very eyes – they ate the people they picked. All the while, they moaned in delight as they chomped and chewed, discussing how *juicy* we are or how *delectable*. One of them even called us a delicacy, and he picked a basket full of us to take back to his village and feed to his neighbors."

While the little people made woeful sounds of mourning, Jacob offered an expression of disgust. It was obvious to his naked eye that these tiny creatures were people and not some mere fruit like an apple or an orange. The people who had feasted on them, he decided, had been savages. He saw fit to assure them that he would not be like them, that he was a kind and goodhearted man.

"That is horrible," he acknowledged and shook his head solemnly. "Such savages should not be allowed out on the loose."

"They should be eaten!" the old balding man shouted, punching his tiny fist into the air. "An eye for an eye!"

"Hear, hear!" shouted several others in agreement.

"They should be hung by their thumbs and whipped with thorny vines until they bleed to death from the wounds!" the old balding one cried out, all fired up.

"By their toes!" added one tiny person, while another yelled out, "Draw and quarter them!"

"Down with the giants!" several began to cry out in unison. "Down with the giants!"

"Wait a minute now," Jacob protested and held his hands up before him. "I have no interest in eating any of ye. I am simply *mystified* by the lot of ya."

"Mystified..." someone whispered. "He be a *witch*!"

"No, silly cow!" one of the women shouted. "A man cannot be a witch. He be a *warlock*!"

"A wizard!" cried out the balding old man. "The man be a wizard, an' he is going to doom us all!"

"No, no!" Jacob proclaimed. "I am merely a man... a

carpenter."

The tiny people silenced and looked at him with big curious eyes. Shyly, one of them who hadn't yet spoken up asked, "What be a *carpenter*?"

Jacob looked at the small person and smiled the warmest, kindest grin he could offer. "I make things out of wood... tables, chairs, really anything someone might need."

"Wood!" the balding old one shouted! "He confesses it! The giant wishes to cut down our tree!"

"No!" one of the tiny women shrieked. "Not our home!"

"No, ye misunderstand," Jacob defended. "I have no intention on cutting down yer tree. In fact, I have no intention on hurting any of ya."

"Ye were going to pick that flower," one of the beings replied. "Ye should take more care with nature!"

Jacob glanced down at the ground to the flower that he was, indeed, going to pick before the strange little voices warned him not to. He bent down to the flower, dusted off its majestic glowing petals, and then stood upright again. Smiling, he looked at the People Tree and motioned for them to look at the flower.

"See, no harm done," he told them proudly. "It's just as healthy and beautiful as before I ever went near it."

Several of the tiny people eyed the flower with scrutiny. The old balding one harrumphed bitterly.

"I have an idea," Jacob said as he noticed the afternoon

light starting to fade. "I must return to my home now, but I shall return to ye again tomorrow, and when I do, I will bring with me a token of my goodwill."

"A token?" said one of the tiny people. "What kind of token?"

Jacob smiled broadly and said, "Ye shall see! For now, I must depart."

He bid the gaggle of tiny stemmed people goodbye and departed their neck of the enchanted forest. As he reached his old reliable relaxation stone, he looked at it and was thankful he hadn't stopped at it as usual. He'd met a remarkable civilization because of his decision – a civilization that hung from the branches of a majestic tree. A great part of him was still amazed and in disbelief over them – and over the entire area in which their tree grew. Another part of him hadn't felt very alone when he was with them. Even though they hadn't been very trusting of him, they'd wanted nothing from him. It had been an interesting and rather enjoyable moment for him, and Jacob was looking forward to experiencing it all over again tomorrow.

"Evening, Jacob," portly Mister Baxter said as they met on the path at the village foot.

"Evening, Mister Baxter," Jacob replied and offered a bright smile.

Pleasantly, he strolled on by before the portly man had an opportunity to ask him anything about work. Just when he was almost out of ear reach, Mister Baxter yelled, "My wife loves the new chairs!"

Jacob sighed and threw a hand up and waved, but he didn't otherwise reply. As far as the village was concerned – as far as the *kingdom* was concerned – he was nothing but a carpenter with nothing else to offer. He knew Mister Baxter's wife loved the four chairs that he crafted for her. He'd been told every time he'd seen either Mister or Missus Baxter since delivering them, and while he was thankful that they liked them, he wished someone would just ask him how his day was instead of always talking about his work.

In his humble home, Jacob found solace once again. He prepared himself a small supper and enjoyed it at the table by the window. He thought of the tiny people hanging from the tree and considered what token of his goodwill he could offer them. When his food was finished, he wandered around his house and then to the workshop out back. While he had made a lot of nice wooden items over the years to give as gifts, everything was a bit too large to consider as a gift to the People Tree.

Thusly, he spent the next several hours in the workshop carving out 100 tiny wooden swords that the little people could hold and defend themselves with, should anyone come around thinking they were food again.

When the last sword was carved and sharpened, he put them all in a basket to bring to them in the morning. Afterward – quite exhausted – he went to bed, where he dreamed of the People

Tree and the majestic area of forest he'd stumbled upon.

The next morning, he awoke refreshed and ready to visit his new acquaintances. He wanted to call them his friends, but friendship was a two-way road and he'd yet to fully earn their trust. He hoped the gifts he bestowed would change that.

There was a bit of work around the shop he'd hoped to muddle through today, but that took second place next to his newest interest. Deciding to take the full day away from work, he gathered his basket of hand-carved goodies and left his home. On the way to the path, he was met with several local villages, all of which greeted him with the same thoughts about his craft that he always received. He tried his best to remain pleasant, but Jacob was too excited to get away from these people to converse with him, so he offered them only quick hellos and goodbyes.

At the edge of the village, he took his usual path and strolled merrily along it. When he reached his relaxation stone, he brushed his hand over it, as if to let it know he hadn't forgotten it and he would soon enjoy its comfort once the time was right and he was ready for rest. The cool rock grew warm to his touch, like it knew every word he said and thoroughly understood each.

Continuing on, the path began to grow darker as it thickened with trees and shrubbery. Then, it began to grow brighter again as the flowers and plants began to shimmer with colorful glows. Jacob sighed pleasantly and smiled as he took in the sights and smells. As for the scent, the air here seemed fresher than any he'd ever breathed.

He was nearing the area of the People Tree, and his excitement was making him giddy. His walk became a trot until he was nearly skipping his way along the narrow path.

"Oiko, doiko, ba dunk dunk dunk," he began as he sang his usual, silly song. "Watch out for the stinky skunk!" He was almost there... just one more bend to turn around, and then he could present his new acquaintances with their special new gifts. "Oiko, doiko, ba dooby do dey! Can ye fly like a rabid blue jay?"

He stopped singing and slowed his steps. A new sound entered his ears. It was a faint sound that sounded like wails and sobs. Curiously, he turned the bend and saw the People Tree.

It was nearly bare of tiny people. Only a few remained on their stems, and each and every one of them was in tears.

"Good heavens!" Jacob exclaimed, shocked by the sight. "What, pray tell, has happened?"

He looked to where the little old balding man resided, but that spot of tree was empty. He was gone.

Upon noticing Jacob, the heavy cries and mournful wails turned into sniffles and groans.

"The others..." one of the few remaining people told him, "they have been taken!"

"Eaten!" screamed a woeful woman. "He was eatin' them as he walked away!"

Jacob gasped, shocked by what he was being told. "Who

did this? Who took the others?" His voice was angered and angst-ridden.

"A portly man!" one of the tiny people said. "With a big fat nose and a curly mustache to hold it up!"

"Mister Baxter!" Jacob said and then gasped again. His anger was now fueled, as he knew who to direct it too. "I promise ye that he shall not get away with this! I shall see to it myself! No… *we* shall see to it ourselves!"

The tiny people looked curiously at one another and then murmured so low that Jacob couldn't hear a word of it. One looked up and over at him and asked, "What *we*? We cannot live off this tree."

"We'll dry up and shrivel!" cried the woeful woman.

"Ye shan't have to leave this tree," he told them and then set the basket on the ground. "But first, I have a gift for ye."

"A gift?" a young one asked curiously from one of the higher branches.

"Aye," said Jacob. Then, he opened the basket and looked inside of it. He had one hundred tiny swords with him – not nearly enough for everyone who had been on the tree. Now, it seemed he had much more than enough, and that saddened him greatly.

One by one, he took the swords and handed them to the tiny people. They fit perfectly into their tiny hands, and the people marveled at them as they wielded them.

"I made these just for ye," he told them, not letting the

pride show in his tone. "Ye may use them to protect thyselves from anyone trying to hurt ye again."

The tiny people were grateful for the offering and accepted their new weapons with as much enthusiasm as they could muster. Jacob wished he'd been able to give them these before Mister Baxter devoured much of their population, but he would see to it that they got to try out their new tools and have some practice before another such dastardly deed could happen in the future.

"Practice with yer new swords," he said to the tiny group. "I must depart, but I shall return within the hour."

"What be an hour?" one of the tiny people asked, confused.

Jacob smiled. It made sense to him that they had no knowledge of man's calculations of time. "Let us just say that I shall return soon, and on this very day."

As the tiny people began to discuss among themselves their new tools for defense, Jacob departed them and started back down the path. He walked briskly, letting his anger fume within him. Once in the village, he ignored every person he came across, refusing eye contact or even a wave of the hand. Hurriedly, he went to his workshop and gathered some supplies in the basket he'd carried back with him.

Then, he set off to Mister Baxter's house, where the portly man and his likewise wife had just finished what they claimed to be the most scrumptious breakfast either had ever eaten.

"Good morning, Jacob!" said the plump man.

"Oh, I just love my new chairs, Jacob!" exclaimed his wife.

"Good morning, Mister Baxter. Missus Baxter." He smiled. It hurt something awful to do so. He felt his teeth gritting against each other through it. "I know this may sound out of the blue, but I am heading into the forest to pick a special variety of flower, and I wonder if ye would like to keep me company."

The husband and wife looked at one another. Jacob continued to smile.

"Oh, what a lovely offer!" Missus Baxter exclaimed.

"I don't know… I have work I could do," said her husband.

"I really hate to go alone," Jacob continued. "I am quite lonely in this village, understand. I have few acquaintances, and I must say, if I do not find someone to talk to here and befriend, I may be forced to move from this lovely village." He sighed, frowned, and lowered his head. His eyes scraped across the table. There, he saw a small bowl filled with tiny hair. He recognized the old balding man's beard in the bowl. The Baxter's had scalped their food before eating it. Jacob's fists clenched beside him. "If ye would like, I could build ye a nice table to go with those new chairs…"

"Oh, a new table!" Missus Baxter cried out, as if she'd just heard the most splendid thing imaginable.

"At no charge?" questioned her husband.

"The only fee would be that of yer company," Jacob told him and smiled again, holding his basket up just a little, "whilst we pick flowers."

Once again, the Baxter's looked at one another. This time, they both smiled. Mister Baxter said, "Well, now. What be we waiting for? Let us pick some flowers!"

Missus Baxter clapped her hands together giddily as the two stood from their seats. They quickly readied themselves, and in a matter of a few short minutes, they were out the front door and alongside Jacob, heading toward his well-worn path.

Conversation was kept light as they walked, and on the path, Jacob saw his relaxation stone come into view.

"I often stop for a rest there," he told the couple and pointed to the large and welcoming stone. "It certainly is a relaxing place."

"I could use a sit," said Missus Baxter. "My feet a sore from all of this walking."

"I know this stone," said her husband. "It *is* relaxing. Shall we have a sit?"

When they reached the stone, Mister Baxter helped his wife onto it, where she sat and relaxed. He climbed up next to her and sat beside her. Then, almost blissfully, they looked off into the beautiful forest.

As they were distracted, Jacob set his basket down and retrieved a heavy mallet. He used it to strike Mister Baxter across the head first, knocking him out. Then, as Missus Baxter began to scream, he slammed the mallet against her skull until he heard it pop and crush, killing her. He returned the mallet to his basket and took out some rope. Quickly, he tied up Mister Baxter's hands and feet, and then tied another long piece around his neck. He fashioned it in such a way that it wouldn't break the man's neck and kill him. Once it was securely tied, he took the length of it and dragged Mister Baxter behind him, all the way to the People Tree.

The forest dimmed. The glowing plants came into view. Soon, he could hear the tiny voices of the tiny people meld with his heavy breathing. When he reached the tree, he saw they were still admiring their new swords, and ones who hung close to one another were even sparring with them.

They hushed when they noticed Jacob's return. Several gasped in shock as they saw him dragging with him the man who had eaten their companions.

"I have brought with me another gift," he told them as he pulled Mister Baxter to the tree.

"It is he!" screamed a tiny woman. "It is the *beast*!"

"Have no fear," Jacob insisted. "I have brought him with me as a gift."

"A gift?" shouted one of the men. "What kind of gift is *he*?"

"The very best kind, as he is bound and breathing." Jacob hoisted the rope over a heavy branch, careful to not strike any of the tiny people with it. "Ye may now avenge yer fallen people."

In a way that would not break Mister Baxter's neck, as the

rope was tied around his fat, he hoisted him up the tree and let him dangle in front of its people.

"Vengeance…" one of them muttered. Then, he seemed to perk up. "Vengeance!" he shouted, and soon the others joined in. "Vengeance! Vengeance!"

From their chanting, Mister Baxter awoke and opened his eyes. He fought against the ropes that bound him and then noticed the tiny people staring at him with their sharp wooden swords aimed right at him.

"What is this?" he demanded and noticed Jacob standing nearby. "What have ye done to me?"

"Ye have committed the worst of crimes," Jacob told his former client. "Ye have eaten people – many people, tiny as they are. Ye plucked them from their home, and ye ate them as if they were fruit."

"They be hanging from stems!" Mister Baxter shouted. The effort caused him to sway on the rope. "They *are* fruit!"

Jacob offered him a warm smile and then looked at the tiny people. "Ye have yer weapons," he said, "and now it be time to slay the giant that wronged you."

Taking a step back so he could fully enjoy the scene, Jacob watched as the group of tiny stemmed people cheered at his command and then began to stab Mister Baxter everywhere and anywhere they could. Seven of them were able to stab him repeatedly in his screaming face, while others attacked his neck, shoulders and stomach.

Eventually, Mister Baxter stopped screaming and the blood ran from him and formed a sloppy puddle on the ground below. When he was assuredly dead - either from the miniscule but multiple wounds riddling his face, neck and stomach, or from the shock of what had happened – Jacob lowered him from the tree and undid the ropes. He then took out a large cutting knife and began to filet the man into small chunks of meat. When there was more than plenty for everyone, he passed portions out to every little person on the tree. Some had to be hoisted up and handed off by others to reach everyone, but eventually, everyone had some and began to eat.

Jacob ate also, deciding it was only fitting for him to take part in the celebration. The meat tasted flavorless to him, although the tiny people seemed to love it. Within a half hour's time, portly Mister Baxter was fully unrecognizable and nothing more than a pulpy ghost of his former self.

"Ye have proven thyself a true friend to us," one of them told him when they were finished with their meal. Jacob smiled as his heart warmed. "Ye shall forever be loved and appreciated by our kind – those of us who hang before ye, and those of us who grow from our branches after."

It was everything that Jacob had ever hoped for. For the first time in a long time, he had true friends – friends that he would cherish for many, many moons to come.

As for the remains of Mister and Missus Baxter, the wife was dragged far beyond the large rock and deep within the forest, where no enchantment lay, and she was buried under a pile of stones. Mister Baxter's remains were buried not far from the People Tree. An unusual thing happened when his bones were laid to rest in the enchanted part of the forest. In a few months time, a tree grew from them. The tree, much like the People Tree, bore the most unique item – branches full of tiny Mister Baxter's. Unlike the People Tree, Jacob ate from the Baxter Tree daily, offering Mister Baxter a taste of what his own cruel hunger had been like.

It is time for fun and games, dearie. Dost thou have a childhood game that ye played and loved? Hide and seek, perhaps? Or mayhap tag?

This story is about a family of siblings that enjoys many of those same games, along with making up new games all of their own. When the average games become mundane, oldest sister invents a brand new one called Rabbit, Rabbit, Where Dost Thou Hop. *Perhaps ye would care to play along? I'll hide and ye can be it!*

Rabbit, Rabbit, Where Dost Thou Hop?

In a tiny cottage just outside a lovely village, Elisabeth was tending to her three younger siblings Maxwell, Wendy, and Tiddleson. When Elisabeth was but sixteen, she and her siblings were orphaned after their parents were eaten by a harpy while fishing from a boat at sea. Raising her siblings was a trying and difficult effort for Elisabeth, but they were good children and usually easy to manage.

She taught them how to clean, chop wood, hunt for food, and even to bake breads and tasty pastry treats. This was often balanced with playtime to keep them happy and to help wear them down so they slept at night. Elisabeth was good at inventing games for them to play. Sometimes, they would play Knights and Dragons, where one of them would be the dragon and others would be the knights, chasing the dragon with sticks serving as swords. If the dragon was poked with the stick, it was slain and whoever poked it won the game.

Another favorite game she invented for the children was Apple High, Apple Low. The children picked a small tree to climb, and one remained on the ground. The one on the ground would try to shake the others out of the short and thin tree, causing the *apples* to drop. If everyone in the tree fell out within five shakes, the shaker was the victor and could then take a turn up in the tree.

Otherwise, the shaker lost the game.

Elisabeth spent much of her free time – which was very little – trying to think of new and exciting games to play with her siblings. Often, they played pretend and acted as if they were kings and queens, lords and ladies, and that their cottage was actually a massive castle filled with wonders and light dangers. While that was a fun way to pass the time, she preferred for them to spend more time outside, in the fresh air and sunlight.

On this day, the children were outside by the small garden, weeding the weeds and picking away bugs from their vegetables and flowers. It was one of their daily chores when it wasn't raining, and it was one that they didn't seem to mind so much. Elisabeth watched them from the window, smiling as they made a game of the chore.

"The dragon is about to eat the royal council!" shouted Matthew as he plucked a caterpillar from a tomato vine.

"The witch has spread poison throughout the land!" cried out Wendy, who took a handful of weeds and plucked them straight out of the ground.

Tiddleson, the youngest of the siblings shouted, "I shall rescue the fair damsel in distress!" He plucked a lady bug off a lettuce leaf and then carried it to the far side of the yard, where he set it free.

Elisabeth chuckled. The children were doing a fine job with the garden, and as that was their last chore for the day, she thought of how to occupy them until it was time for food and rest. They had played their games so many times that they were becoming bored with them. She tried to think of a new game and decided to base one off a poem her mother told her when she was younger.

"When things do not seem to be going yer way," her mother had said, "Yell *Rabbit, Rabbit* for good luck all day."

While it was not luck that Elisabeth was thinking or, nor did she hope to entertain the children with short poetry, the recollection managed to help her think of a new game.

She left her place at the window and stepped outside as the children finished their gardening chores. When they were done, she gave them each an apple for their efforts, along with a mug of water.

"What shall we do now?" Wendy asked when their snacks were finished.

"Shall we play Apple High, Apple Low?" Matthew inquired.

"I don't want to play Apple High, Apple Low," said Tiddleson in a pout. "I'm too small. I can never shake thee from the tree!"

Elisabeth chuckled and said, "How about we play a new game today?"

Her siblings were excited over this suggestion. Eagerly, they asked what new game it would be.

"We shall play a brand-new game called Rabbit, Rabbit,

Where Dost Thou Hop," she told them in an energetic tone. "One of us shall be *it* whilst the others hide."

"But that sounds like Hide and Seek," said Matthew.

"It is similar, but in this version, the one who is *it* wears a blindfold over their eyes."

"A blindfold?" asked Wendy.

"Yes, and the other's hide. The one who's *it* will yell, 'Rabbit! Rabbit!' and those hiding will yell, 'Where dost thou hop?' The one who is *it* will have to follow the others' voices to find them. The first one they find becomes the new *it*!"

The children were intrigued by this version of the age-old game of Hide and Seek. Their excitement was evident, but they insisted Elisabeth be *it* for the first run.

"Why must I be *it*?" she asked, although she didn't mind being the first one to play the part.

"Because yer the biggest of us!" Tiddleson exclaimed.

"Because yer the oldest!" added Matthew.

"Because it's yer game," she was informed by Wendy.

Elisabeth laughed pleasantly. "Okay," she said. "I shall grab a scarf to use as a blindfold and we will begin."

She chose a scarf and then led the children toward the foot of the forest to play their game.

"Okay," she began after she tied the scarf around her head to blind her. "I shall count to twenty and give ye all a chance to hide, but remember the rules. When I yell 'Rabbit, Rabbit,' ye must yell 'Where dost thou hop.' Don't go too far though. The forest can be dangerous."

The children excitedly agreed and, as she began to count, she could hear them giggle as they ran and found their hiding places.

"Eleven..." she said, halfway through her slow count. "Twelve..." She could still hear them squealing pleasantly as they hid; their voices were a bit further away now. "Seventeen... Eighteen..." At 'twenty,' she smiled and spun around in a circle. Then, she shouted, "Rabbit! Rabbit!"

"Where dost thou hop?" she heard her three siblings shout from their respective hiding places. Their voices were coming from her left. Giddily, she turned toward them and began to carefully walk.

She walked for a few moments and the giggling stopped. Where were they, she wondered as she turned slightly to her left and then to her right.

"Rabbit! Rabbit!" she called again, smiling from ear to ear.

For a short moment, no one said anything. Then, from a bit further away than they sounded before, she heard her siblings yell, "Where dost thou hop?"

One of them sounded close. She believed it to be Tiddleson, and she ambled blindly toward where his voice came from. There, she heard his distinct giggling. Quickly, she reached forward to tag him but swiped over the leaves of a bush instead.

Feeling all around, she couldn't find her brother anywhere.

"No fair moving from yer places!" she yelled, a bit frustrated.

"No one has moved!" she heard Matthew call from several meters to her right.

Quickly, she turned in his direction. "Rabbit! Rabbit!"

"Where dost thou hop?" called the children, but now their voices seemed even further away than before.

Elisabeth was tempted to remove the blindfold from over her eyes and catch her siblings in the act of cheating at the game, but she decided instead to continue on. If they were cheating, she would simply give them extra chores tomorrow, and there would be no games to break the day up.

A little faster than before, she walked toward the direction that Wendy's voice had come from. She held her hands out before her to make sure she didn't run smack dab into a tree or anything else. In a few more steps, she felt the bark of a tree and paused.

"Rabbit! Rabbit!" she called again. Patiently, she awaited their response.

"Where dost thou hop?"

They almost sounded like an echo this time. She swallowed to see if her ears were suddenly clogged, but they were not. Once again, she was tempted to remove the blindfold and look to see if her siblings were tricking her by running further away. She decided to give them one last opportunity before ruining her new game.

She walked for a while more, feeling all around her to ensure her safety and to feel for her siblings. When she felt like she'd walked a decent length, she shouted again, "Rabbit! Rabbit!"

"Where dost thou hop?" she heard voices call from far behind her. How had she passed them by already? It made no sense to her, but nonetheless, Elisabeth turned around and headed back.

Suddenly, she heard giggling, but like the game question before it, it was coming from behind her again, in the direction from which she'd just turned. Now, she knew her siblings were making a fool of her. They were intentionally leading her around in circles, and she was growing perturbed.

Finally, she stopped and took off the scarf from around her eyes. She'd expected the sunlight to hit her and distort her vision, but after a couple of blinks, she could see fine.

The first thing Elisabeth noticed was that she was standing in a thick part of the forest and surrounded by trees. Next, as she turned in a circle, she saw that her small cottage was nowhere to be seen. Gazing through the trees and small shrubs scattered over the ground, she sought her siblings. They, too, were nowhere to be seen.

She swallowed somewhat nervously and fidgeted where she stood. Then, she took a deep breath and looked up at the sky. It was mid-afternoon when she and her siblings began her new game. Now, after just a few short moments of it, the sky was growing darker. It felt impossible to her for so much time to have passed.

"Rabbit…" she called in an unsure tone. "Rabbit…"

She waited for the reply, but it never came. Elisabeth took a few steps in what she believed to be the direction from whence she came. Then, she stopped again and listened.

In a voice a bit louder than before, she called again, "Rabbit! Rabbit!"

"Where dost thou hop?" she heard from behind her, and with a jerk, she turned toward the voice. Yet, there was no one there.

Frustrated, she straightened her shoulders and shouted as loudly as she could, "Rabbit! Rabbit!"

"Where dost thou hop?" came the reply, this time from up above. Were her siblings in the treetops? That was another impossibility, as Tiddleson was terrified of heights and thusly never climbed trees.

Still, she looked upward to the treetops and let her eyes roam through them. The dimming sky made it difficult for her to spot anyone or anything.

"Okay!" she finally shouted and steered her vision back from the treetops. "I give up! Where ye be hiding?"

"Right behind ye," said that voice that sounded similar to Matthew's… but not quite.

Elisabeth became nervous again. She hesitated and took a slow breath. Then, uneasily, she began to turn around. There, nearly a dozen meters away, was Matthew. He looked strange. His stance was slouched. His head was up but his eyes were closed and his jaw was hanging open. When she looked at his feet, Elisabeth noticed they dangled above the ground.

"Ye still must tag me," Matthew said. His mouth moved like a puppet's mouth. His voice was still queer and a little croaky.

All of the sudden, she heard her sister Wendy from nearby. Jerking her head to the right, Elisabeth saw Wendy standing approximately the same distance away from her that Matthew was. "Where dost thou hop?" Wendy asked. Her voice was similar to Matthew's – not quite right and not all there.

"Where dost thou hop?" It was Tiddleson this time, far to her left, standing just like the others. Elisabeth was no longer sure she could even consider this standing – not when their feet weren't touching the ground.

She looked back at Matthew and squinted to see him better. She gazed at his dangling feet and noticed something behind them – something that seemed almost like two more feet…

"Rabbit…" Matthew said. His voice had changed a little since just before. It was deeper.

"Rabbit…" said Wendy. Her voice was similar and less feminine now.

"Rabbit…" Tiddleson added. She looked at him as his body dropped and revealed a wicked dwarf. An impish smile crossed over its lips.

Gasping, she looked to Matthew, who also dropped to the ground, and then to Wendy, who followed suit. Behind each stood another dwarf.

They were brutish looking creatures with thick beards, pointy ears, beady eyes, and long black hats that drooped behind them. Although they were each no bigger than Elisabeth's youngest sibling, they were strong and had knuckles that nearly dragged the ground.

All at once, the drafts retrieved their pickaxes from the bags hung from their shoulders. Each then slammed their picks into the back of the siblings' heads and slowly began to approach Elisabeth, dragging the children along behind them.

Elisabeth shrieked horribly and began to back up. Then, she turned from them all and ran. Her siblings were dead, and she couldn't understand how this had happened. They had been playing a simple game around the yard, and now, they had picks lodged in their skulls and Elisabeth was running through an area of the forest that she did not recognized and had likely never been in.

There hadn't been a dwarf sighting in the area for nearly a century. Elisabeth was sure of that much. The dwarves had been long exiled from the kingdom and forced to live in the caves at the far end of the forest. Yet, the far end of the forest was much too far away from her cottage for her to have reached during this simple game. The area was forbidden to anyone in the kingdom from entering. No one ever dared.

She had no time to question it any further. She had to run and escape.

Glancing behind her, she could not see if the dwarves were in pursuit or not. It was darker out now, and she knew that it would soon be night, as strange as that seemed to her.

Elisabeth suddenly hit hard against a thick dirt and rock formation, smacking into it and falling back dazed. She shook it off and stood unsteadily. Her vision took a moment to focus on what was before her. She placed a hand to it and felt it. It felt like a wall of sorts. Dragging her hand along it, she walked until it touched to a large opening. Suddenly, she realized she was at a cave.

With little choice, she slipped inside of it and was shrouded in utter darkness. The air felt a little damp here, and as she walked, her feet became damp as well. She was afraid to walk fast through here, as she worried of tripping or stumbling. She also had no idea of where she was going or how large or small the cave was. In fact, as far as Elisabeth knew, she could have just trapped herself in here for the dwarves to find and kill.

She walked further, relieved to have not hit another wall. Instead, she came to a slope that sent her tumbling down to where there was light. When she landed, she stood in the magical glow of a mine filled with enigma diamonds. Her eyes lit up at the sight. Never before had she seen such a display of marvelous beauty and wonderment. The enigma diamond was one of the most precious and rare gemstones in all of the land. With two of them placed strategically anywhere in the world, one could travel from one spot to another just by stepping over them. They acted as portals, and it finally dawned on her as to how she ended up in the forbidden part of the forest.

Portals had been placed by the wicked dwarves, and she and her siblings had all crossed over one.

Elisabeth strained her mind to formulate a plan. Beyond this mine, she saw the path continued. Legend had it that if one took two enigma diamonds and clanked them together, it would activate them and link them to one another. Hurriedly, she clawed through a bit of hard dirt and pulled two diamonds free. Then, wishing hard for the legend to be true, she slammed them together in her hands. A reverberating tremble came from the enigma diamonds and rippled throughout Elisabeth's body. Her ears began to hurt as a sharp buzzing sound made itself known. This sound was accompanied by a striking pain that overwhelmed her body.

She nearly dropped the stones but the moment of these sensations quickly ended. Relieved, her concern fell back to the enigma diamonds and if the legend had been true.

She placed one on the ground a few meters up, and then she walked back a few meters and placed the other at her feet. With a deep and hopeful breath, she stepped over the stone. Miraculously, she appeared in front of the second one.

"Rabbit! Rabbit!" she heard the evil dwarves call as they

hunted her through the cave. "Rabbit! Rabbit!"

Their voices were echoes, letting her know they were not incredibly close. Likely, they knew of the slope and would be more careful going down it, therefore taking longer than she had.

With a coy grin, she picked up the two linked enigma diamonds and shouted, "Where dost thou hop?" as loudly as she could.

Then, hurriedly, she continued down the path, carrying the glowing diamonds with her. They lit her path as she swiftly walked, and soon, she could see moonlight through an exit. Once outside of the tunnel, she dug a small hole in the ground and buried one of enigma diamonds in it. She then sought for a good location to plant the other one.

Water could be heard nearby and she rushed to the source. Thanks to the light of the remaining diamond, she was able to stop before she stepped over a ledge that dropped down to the rocky sea below. In that very spot, she planted that second diamond.

Not far from that spot, Elisabeth hid in the shadows of the trees and waited. It was only a matter of time before she saw the dwarves appear in front of the second stone, where they instantly fell to their watery graves.

They had not had her siblings in tow. Likely, they'd abandoned them when Elisabeth began to run, knowing the children would slow them down.

She went to the spot where the enigma diamond was buried

and retrieved it. Then, she returned to the tunnel and collected the second one. She took several more from within the mine, carrying all she could and connecting one to the smallest one of all so that she would remember which one it was. This smallest diamond, she would secure at her cottage. The other, she buried in the mine so that she would be able to find it again if she ever needed.

When she found the location of her dead siblings, she connected two more enigma diamonds and buried one where they lay. When she finally reached her cottage and the sun was high in the sky, she took the other stone and set it by the garden. Then, she stepped through the portal and back thrice, collecting her siblings and laying them out in the yard to be buried.

With her siblings no longer alive to care for, Elisabeth found a new life for herself – one where she was able to benefit from the extravagant enigma diamonds. By placing them all throughout the village, and even throughout the kingdom, she was able to transport to locations that would have otherwise taken her hours or days to reach by foot. One such stone she hid in the village marketplace so that she could transport from there straight into her cottage and back again.

It was through this carelessness that she was spotted vanishing into thin air by the baker's wife, who reported the incident to the King. Poor Elisabeth was collected by the royal guards in the middle of the night whilst she slept. The next morning, she was deemed a witch by the King and sentenced to immediate death by hanging. Her death was swift and her body swayed from the rope for three days as a warning to any other witches that may have resided within the kingdom.

I hope ye enjoyed the game, dearie, because within this next tale are no fun or games. It is, instead, the story of a father and daughter, burned at the stake by a King in mourning. It may sound like the tragic way a story should end, but this is the way this dark tale begins.

There is a curse now spreading across the kingdom, and sometimes the only way to end such a thing is by making amends to the one you've wronged. As the King will find out, that is not so simple when the one you've wronged is dead. This is The Scent of Abraham Eleventh.

The Scent of Abraham Eleventh

Abraham Eleventh was a prominent man within the village until one day, when the King's buggy rode through, his small daughter ran out in the middle of the path. The horse reared up, setting the buggy unbalanced. Abraham's daughter was nearly trampled by the spooked animal, but her death was thwarted by her father's swift action.

Heroically, he hurried to her and pulled her away from the horse, thusly saving her life. The King's buggy was not so fortunate. The horse managed to break away from it and the buggy flipped and rolled onto its side. While the King had not been in the buggy, his Queen and their infant son had been. The Queen survived, but the baby died.

Devastated over the death of the throne's only heir, the King blamed Abraham Eleventh for the actions of his daughter and sentenced him to death by burning. Normally, a good old-fashioned hanging was the preferred method of execution in the kingdom, but the King wanted Abraham to suffer and to feel the pain as the fire engulfed him.

Deciding that the little girl was no more innocent than her father, she too was sentenced to death and tied with her father at the stake, surrounded by dry hay to feed the flames. Abraham begged for his daughter's release, pleading with the King and his executioner that her actions in the village had been accidental and she'd meant no harm.

The King would not hear his pleas. Thusly, at high noon, a torch was thrown onto the hay and a great fire ignited. Abraham's daughter began screaming first as the flames ate into their flesh and stemmed unbearable pain throughout them; Abraham held his tears and screams at bay. Instead, he looked down at his precious young daughter and stared in shock and horror as she burned alive before his very eyes. Her screams were short lived, and he watched his daughter die.

Finally, he released a mournful howl that left his body so loudly it made the noses of everyone present bleed. As Abraham died, his howl finally ended. In that same moment, every child in the kingdom fell dead to the ground.

The bodies of Abraham Eleventh and his young daughter continued to burn until they were nothing but bones and teeth. The stench was strong from the moment he died – unbearable, in fact. It burned its way into the noses of everyone present, even as they tried to tend to the sudden deaths of their many children.

After a while when the fire was out and the smoldering ashes and remains had cooled, caretakers were sent to clean up the mess and dispose of the bones. When they reached the site, the bones of the little girl were there, but those of her father were not. They did the job the best they could, removing the girl's bones from the site, grinding them up, and letting them go with the wind. Then, they reported their findings to the King.

The King decided that this was an intentional theft by somebody within his kingdom. So, on the day of the mass funeral for the village's dead children, an announcement was made of the missing bones and a reward was offered for anyone who could return them to the King, along with the person who had stolen them.

This caused a stirring of murmurs and discussion between the villagers. The funeral services abruptly ended, and nearly everyone present began to question each other over where they were when the bones disappeared. When no one confessed to the crime, the group departed and returned to their homes or businesses.

In the night, a familiar smell overcame the village air and seeped its way into the nostrils of all the sleeping villagers. It was the very same scent that they'd smelled while Abraham Eleventh and his daughter burned at the stake. It awoke every one of them from their slumber and led them from their beds. Once outdoors, each discovered that their livestock and other animals had all died, and this was the case throughout the village.

A special meeting was held on the village square the following morning. It was decided that there was not only a thief on the land, but a murderer of animals as well. The scent of Abraham could not be explained, but they related it to the dead animals to end the discussion.

A new spark was lit within the villagers, and despite the reward, they became more eager to hunt down the vile person who was terrorizing their land before that person could do anymore damage. Throughout the day, armed guards were sent to each and every home, where they questioned everybody present in each. No one admitted to being the one behind the crimes. Each had an alibi of where they were when the bones were taken, and most admitted to being asleep when the animals died.

With the search unsuccessful, the village went to bed fearful that the horrible monster would strike again.

When they awoke, they discovered they had been right. Throughout the kingdom, it was discovered that every crop had burned and died during the night. Every garden, every flower, every herb and blade of grass had perished the same, leaving the kingdom in a barren state. Without livestock for meat, grains and vegetables, the food supply was suddenly scarce. The air surrounding every bit of nature's demise held the same scent of death from Abraham's burning.

This not only frightened the people, but it mystified and confused them as well. There was no way that everything could have burned overnight without anyone noticing, and it was even more unlikely that one person could have committed the crime. Witchcraft was the most likely answer, it was decided, and the King ordered every suspected witch in the kingdom to be hung.

Several women met their deaths at the hands of the executioner that very afternoon, thusly ridding the kingdom of the black magic plaguing them.

With the King and his kingdom now content that their sudden curse was over, the villagers went about the rest of their day in a lighter and relieved way. That night, they slept peacefully, sleeping off the exhaustion of the recent trying events. In the morning, screams echoed throughout the kingdom as each pregnant woman awoke to a miscarriage. The air surrounding each of these devastated mothers held the pungent scent of burn and decay... the scent of death that had formed from the burning bodies of Abraham Eleventh and his daughter.

For the rest of this day, there was quiet in the village. Most people remained home, and in the castle, a special council convened with the King and Queen to discuss the latest horrid events.

It was recalled that the first time the scent was smelled was at that eventful burning. It was also the moment that the first of the events happened – the sudden death of all the children. The second unusual event was the disappearance of Abraham Eleventh's bones. Next, every animal in the kingdom met the same fate as the children had, followed by the loss of everything that grew from soil and dirt. Now, every expected child was dead, aborted from the wombs of their mothers.

The council argued that the curse extended much deeper

than merely women suspected as witches. They decided that wizards were also in play, and under the King's orders, the few scholars in the kingdom were gathered and executed.

Sleep was uneasy throughout the night as everyone seemed to wait to see if this recent cleansing of the wicked had ended their curse. In the morning, they discovered that all water in the kingdom, from streams to creeks to wells and springs, was black and thick like tar. The water in troughs, buckets, tubs, and containers was the same.

Panic began to grow among the people. They began to hoard what little supplies they had left – food, wine, ales. Some began to fight with others to convince them into sharing their supplies, but this caused a bloodbath. All over the kingdom, people began to kill one another for a loaf of bread or a pint of dark ale. By nightfall, the population had dwindled greatly, and those who remained stayed awake that night, protecting what supplies they had left.

The King was one of those awake all night. He stood at the large open window of his room, staring out the castle and at his kingdom in turmoil. He had done everything advised to end this great curse, and each had failed. Now, his people were slaying one another merely to stay alive. Whatever was happening, this slaughter was a direct result of it.

Standing at the window, he took in a deep breath. The scent smelled like it always did when one of these horrible events was happening. It smelled of Abraham Eleventh and his daughter, burning alive at the stake.

In this moment, the King thought of his infant son – the former heir to the throne, dead and in a glass coffin, prominently displayed in the castle's mourning room. He looked at his wife, who had somehow managed to fall asleep despite the fear and chaos. She was beautiful, and he worried what this would do to her.

The King then left his bedchamber and walked quietly to the mourning room, where he spent the rest of the night watching his baby as if the boy was simply asleep.

Just before the sun rose, he smelled that horrid smell once more. Only this time, it was not wafting up to him through a window. It was coming from within the mourning room. He looked from his child to the glass and watched it begin to crack. The crack spread through the glass like a spider web. Then, it suddenly stopped.

The King stared in wonder at it for a moment. Then, with a shaky finger, he touched it.

The glass shattered from his touch, spraying throughout the room in tiny splinters and cutting into his hand, face, and clothes. While the fresh wounds stung and even though several of the splinters were embedded in his lips and his eyelids from where he'd closed his eyes, his focus was on his child.

Horrified and shocked into a silent stillness, the King

watched as his dead son began to burn before his very eyes. There was no fire to be seen, but the flesh and hair began to burn and melt away, charring the child and burning within it. All too swiftly, the baby burned to a crisp and then turned to dust… all but his bones.

Brought back to his functions, the King stood quickly and backed away from the tiny skeleton. Now, he knew the cause of these events had nothing to do with witches or wizards or thieves or animal killers. It was Abraham Eleventh, himself. He was the cause of all of this; the King was certain of it.

Turning away from the sight of this seventh uncanny event, the King hurried from the room and retreated down to the cellar, where he calmed himself with a bottle of wine. When it was finished and he returned to the main entrance foyer, he found his wife standing at the open door, staring out at the world.

He joined her at her side. The castle was not enormous and it sat atop a small hill overlooking the village and the land surrounding the kingdom. From the village, he could hear faint screaming and wailing cries.

Ordering his wife to stay inside, the King gathered his guards and ventured with them down the hill to the foot of the village. He worried that they were killing one another again, but when he got there, he saw that he was wrong.

Many small skeletons were laid out on the ground at the village square. They were the skeletons of the children they'd buried at the mass funeral following Abraham's burning. The King quickly learned that the villagers had been awakened by the horrid scent and followed it to the square. There, they discovered the children's bodies. Upon the discovery, the bodies began to burn away – just as the King's own infant son had.

He explained his theory to them of the curse of Abraham Eleventh. When once such a theory would have been laughed at and ridiculed, it now seemed fully accepted.

The problem was that no one knew what to do about it. All seemed doomed.

The King then offered the bones of the children to Abraham's spirit and begged the apparition for peace and to restore the water and earth to the kingdom.

No sign came alerting the King or his people that his wishes had been heard. Neither was there a sign of acceptance of the offering or even forgiveness. However, nothing else bad seemed to happen in that moment and the King saw that as a good sign.

For the rest of the day and into the early evening, the people remained at the stake with the bones of the children, wondering what would happen with them. Would they be taken? Collected by the vengeful specter? Would they remain there until they – like Abraham's daughter's bones – finally became dust?

When the sun began to set, everyone returned to their dwellings, including the exhausted King. He was greeted upon his return by his wife. The Queen kissed him fondly on the cheek and led him to the grand dining room, where they feasted on what could be found and drank heavily from their royal supply of wine.

At bedtime, they lay together and drifted off to heavy and worn out sleep. In the morning, the King awoke, but the Queen did not. She did not look like herself either. She looked ancient and withered like a mummy. The air held the stench of cursed death that the kingdom had come to know.

Panicked, the King ripped himself from the bed and stumbled toward the window. He pressed a hand against its ledge. The other clasped against his heart as he stared at his dead wife.

He barely dressed before he fled the room. Outside of his castle, he heard many mournful cries fill the air from the village below the hill. Stunned from seeing the state of his wife, he staggered down the hill and to the village, where the cries became louder.

As it happened, every woman in the kingdom was dead and withered. This was another of Abraham Eleventh's curses... his *events*. Of this, the King was certain.

The bodies of the women were dragged to the same spot as the bones of the children. In a pile around the stake, the women were placed atop the bones. As the King saw it, Abraham Eleventh had taken the very souls of these women. He may as well have their bodies too.

Now, all that remained were the adult males of the

kingdom. There were no more women or children, animals or crops… no clean water to drink or bathe in… It was a situation that the King never thought imaginable.

To help console his remaining people, he ordered them to his castle, where they would stay for the remainder of the day and throughout the night. He explained that there was some food, although it would have to be rationed, and there was wine, ale, and scotch. This lifted their spirits as much as their spirits could be lifted, and in a defeated line, they filed up the hill and into the castle.

Once the men had some bread in their stomachs and some liquor in their mugs, they began to calm. The King did his best to help ease the tension of their impossible situation, but even though the men were calmer, they were no more accepting of the situation than they had been. A few demanded that they set out on foot and leave this kingdom and its curse behind. Others insisted they needed to find Abraham Eleventh's bones and put them to rest in burial. A handful believed there was no hope – that no matter what they did or where they went, the curse would follow them and they would be doomed.

The King did not know what to believe. While everything was so incredibly dire that – yes – he did feel like they were doomed, he refused to accept the feeling. There had to be a way to undo what was done. For the first time, he deeply considered his harsh punishment of Abraham and his daughter. Surely, what happened had been an accident. The child had not intended to spook the horse. The King's son had not been murdered in cold blood. The toppling of the carriage had killed him. His forehead had slammed too hard against something. Abraham had been right to plea for his daughter's life, and now the King fully understood this.

He decided that he would return to the spot of Abraham's death in the morning and explain his realization to him. He would beg for forgiveness, and he would beg for his kingdom to be restored. It was the only thing he knew of to do, and even if it didn't work, he had to clear his conscience of what he did and confess his misjudgment in the sentencing.

The hour grew later and the men, drunken on their ale, liquor and wine, fell fast asleep in their chairs – exhausted from the events. The King decided to sleep in the same room, and he found a corner where he quickly drifted off.

When he awoke, he did so to the familiar scent of Abraham Eleventh. Instantly, he knew something was tragically wrong. Standing from his spot on the floor, he looked around the room. Every man there was long dead; only skeletons in clothing remained.

That was the last of his people. He was no longer a King, he realized. He was now nothing more than the last man standing.

He left the room, left the castle, and walked down the hill to the village. It was a deserted ghost town – lonely and desolate.

He let a single tear run down his cheek. It was all he could muster; the events had made him numb.

Slowly, the defeated King made his way to the site of Abraham's burning. The bodies of the women and the bones of the children were still there. He knelt down before them and stared at the terrible and saddening sight. With nowhere else to go or nothing else to do, he remained there all day. Not once did he consider food or fluids. He did not sleep or grow impatient. He simply stayed on his knees in front of the bodies and mourned his fallen kingdom.

When the sun set, he returned to his castle. It no longer felt like home to him. It was meant for both his comfort and his protection. It now provided neither of those things.

At the top of the hill, he turned to face the village one more time, in hope that he would see something that would restore his sense of self. Instead, he felt a rumble across the land, and before his very eyes, he watched the ground open up and swallow his village whole. When all was gone except for the King and his castle, the ground closed up again and the land was barren of any semblance that a village had ever been there.

The King could not believe what he saw. It was gone... truly gone. Not a single structure remained, and it was now official – he was a King no more, as he hadn't even a village to rule over any longer.

Entering into his castle, he went up to his bedchamber and

the bed that he'd shared with his Queen. Atop the bed, he lay straight and closed his eyes, wondering if it was possible to simply sleep one's self to death.

The King succeeded in drifting off to sleep, but he did not succeed in dying from it. Instead, he was awakened by an eerie feeling and a familiar smell.

What was left, he wondered, for this apparition to take from him? Abraham Eleventh's curse had already claimed everything. There was nothing left. Nothing of any *true* value. Anything that had mattered was already gone.

The moon was full in the sky and its bright light lit the King's bedchamber with an almost ethereal glow. To his left, his closed door creaked open. He propped himself up on his elbows and stared at it.

From the shadows of the hall, the King watched as a skeleton in a black cloak entered the room. Smoke rose from it and wafted out from the opening of the cloak. Whilst he normally would have expected the Reaper to have been the bearer of those bones, he knew differently. Those were the missing bones of Abraham Eleventh. He had reclaimed them, and now, he'd come to claim the King.

The King did not expect mercy from the entity, nor did he expect forgiveness. Yet, he told Abraham Eleventh what he'd discovered within himself. He told of how sorry he was over the punishment he'd put forth to him and his young daughter. He admitted to acting out of anger and grief over his lost son – the dead infant heir to the throne. No longer did he beg for his kingdom to be restored. The time for that was done and gone. Now, he only wished for his own suffering to end.

Abraham Eleventh approached the King at his bed. Slowly, he lifted a skeletal hand and pointed a bony finger at him. Then, with a quick and slight touch, he poked him on his forehead. While normally bones would have held a coolness to them, this skeletal finger's touch burned like fire. The King began to scream through the pain. Abraham Eleventh took a step back and watched.

The King's flesh and clothing began to burn away, although there was no actual flame to be seen. Just as Abraham and his daughter had burned at the stake, the invisible fire ate through the King in the same manner, and taking the same painstakingly long time to do so. The King's screaming cries changed to gurgled gasps and, finally, a plea for help. Abraham Eleventh shook his hooded head *no*.

For the remainder of the few moments of life he had left, the King silenced and stared into the eyeless sockets of the man he'd wrongfully executed. When he was finally dead, the invisible fire continued to burn him until all that remained was a skeleton atop a bed.

With the King properly punished for his wrongful doings, Abraham Eleventh's skeleton fell apart. His bones and the cloak that had shielded them tumbled down to the floor in a disarrayed pile. A final bit of smoke wafted up from them, and then they cooled.

Would ye like a spot of tea to calm yer nerves? I can see yer a bit shaken by that last tale. Understandably so. Revenge can be a nasty thing!

Our next story will perhaps offer ye a bit of hope after that moment of darkness. It is the oldest story of them all. Man meets woman. Man and woman fall in love. Woman becomes blessed with the man's child. The child is born from an egg.

Wait... what? That's not the way the old story goes? Well then, yer surely in for a treat. Perhaps ye might even discover a happily ever after within the House of Snakes.

House of Snakes

There once was a house in the forest that was as old as the village it was built near. The house was built by a reclusive man that had not wished to live under a new King's rule. He built his house to be small and humble, out of supplies he found nearby. It allowed for him a peaceful existence in which he enjoyed years of solitude.

In his fortieth year, a strange woman dressed in a garment of white silk knocked on his door. Upon the first gaze into her hypnotic green eyes, he fell in love. Together, they had a child, but this was no ordinary child, and the way it was born had frightened the man. His child had been laid as an egg and hatched right before his very eyes.

In the night, the man murdered his love in her sleep, knowing that she was a demonic beast and thusly had to die. When he tried to kill the child, he discovered that he could not. While she had been born from a serpent demon, she was made of him as well. Her flesh, eyes, and form were amazingly human. The man decided to keep and raise his daughter, and as she grew, he withheld any knowledge of her true origin from her.

On the eve of his daughter's sixteenth birthday, the man walked into his daughter's room to find her sitting atop a nest of seven eggs. From her serpent mother and her human father, she had self-fertilized herself and laid the eggs. Perched atop them, she looked up at her father, terrified and in tears over her confusion of what had happened.

Trying to raise his daughter without knowledge of what she really was had not worked. She was still cursed, like her mother had been. The man retrieved his axe and killed his daughter. Once she was dead, he pushed her body to the floor and smashed the eggs with his heavy foot.

Unable to handle what had happened and what he had done, the man gathered a rope and a chair and carried them out to a nearby tree. There, he hung himself.

While he had thought he'd crushed all of the eggs, he had missed one – an eighth egg that had fallen off the nest. As it was summer, the egg was kept warm within the house, and eventually, it hatched. Another beautiful baby girl was born.

As she rolled from the egg, she hit against the wooden leg of a chair. This slight jolt caused her to take her first breath of air. With it, she began to cry. Her cries were loud and scared, and they sounded through the house and out into the forest. While no human heard them, their vibrations were noticed by the many snakes that resided nearby. Slithering from their domains to the house were snakes of all shapes, sizes and colors. They were drawn to the child, and once inside, they embraced her as one of them.

When winter arrived, the house became cold. In order to protect the baby, a barrier of snakes covered each and every space of the house's structure, inside and out. The infant survived the winter, but the snakes shielding the house did not. They froze into ice and turned the house into ice with them.

It happened about that time that a young woman came upon the frozen house of snakes. She could hear the baby within it, but she saw no way to enter. With a wave of her hand, she made the door open. Curiously, she stepped inside and felt the cold. On the floor in the middle of the room, she saw the baby, wrapped in snakes to keep warm.

How the child was alive in such cold seemed impossible to her. She approached the infant girl and knelt down before her. The snakes embracing her reared their heads back and hissed. Their forked tongues flapped at her in warning.

The woman smiled and waved her hand over them. The snakes relaxed and untangled themselves from around the child. Then, they parted so that the woman could lift the cold but seemingly healthy little girl into her arms.

"There, there," said the woman to the baby as she cradled her against her bosom. "Silence yer tears, precious one."

The woman laid the child atop the dusty and cold bed and stepped from the house. Gazing at the frozen snakes that had shielded it and died to save the child's life, she performed a magical spell that turned them and the house into a sturdy, wooden structure. This made the snakes appear to be carved into the wood, giving it a magnificent and original façade. Doing so also made it more secure from the elements, and as she stepped inside, she noticed the significant difference.

She chose this house as her new dwelling and raised the little girl as her own, allowing the child's snake family to remain with them. Eventually, old and gray, there was no magic in the world that could rescue the woman from her fate. She died, leaving the girl behind. The child was a woman of twenty by this time, and with just her snake family to keep her company, she grew hungry for human companionship.

"I must leave ye for a time," she told the serpents as they gathered around her. "There is more beyond this forest, and I must explore it. Please, take care, friends. I shall one day return to ye."

And so, the young woman set forth to discover human companionship, leaving her house of snakes behind.

Many days and nights went by, and as weeks turned to months, the young woman did not return to her house. The snakes grew weary, feeling that the worst must have happened to her. Eventually, the door to the house opened once again, but it was not the young woman who entered. Instead, it was a somewhat older woman who looked very similar to the one they'd helped raise. The older woman was pregnant and had a man with her.

"I told ye I would return!" she exclaimed as she entered the house. Her companioned gasped behind her at what he saw. Looking to him, she said, "Do not be shy, Lord Jameson. This is my family. They shan't hurt ye."

Regardless of what she told him, Lord Jameson took a great step back as every snake in the room lifted its head and hissed at him. He was terrified.

"Please, do come in," she beckoned and held the door for him.

The lord was hesitant to follow through. He stood outside the doorway for a long moment, staring at the many snakes that were almost daring him to enter and become their feast.

"We should return to the village," he told her. "I – I cannot stay here."

"Nothing here shall hurt ya," the pregnant woman said. Looking at the snakes, she asked, "Will ye?"

The snakes lowered themselves and ceased their hissing. Still, their eyes never left Lord Jameson.

Over the next few weeks, the lord became used to having the snakes around, and they did not strike at him even once during that time. However, when the woman drew close to the time of relieving her pregnancy, the lord suggested the snakes depart the house for the sake of the baby. The woman refused and insisted that the serpents were her family and that they would remain to protect the child.

Although he agreed to her decision, Lord Jameson waited for her to go to sleep that night. Then, with his mighty sword, he slaughtered each of the snakes within the house. Before the woman awoke the next morning, he removed all remnants of the snakes from the house and hid them deep within the forest. Then, as quietly as he could, he climbed into bed with her and slept.

When the woman noticed her snakes were gone, Lord Jameson claimed that they simply were not needed any longer, as he was there now to protect and care for her and the child. He explained that they left on their own over night, while she slept so that there wouldn't be a fuss over their departure.

The woman mourned the loss of her beloved snakes. She slept for most of the day nearly every day for weeks. Nothing Lord Jameson did could keep her awake or out of bed for very long. Perhaps she was no longer whole, and perhaps the birth of their child could fill the void left by the snakes.

When the special day arrived, a hole was dug in the earth just outside of the house. There, the woman squatted and pushed, working out of her the new life she'd carried for so long. On a hard and long push, a large whitish egg came out of her with an umbilical cord attached. Tears of joy covered her cheeks as she exhaled and celebrated the miracle of life.

Lord Jameson, however, was not so pleased. He was shocked and horrified by what he saw, and clumsily, he stumbled backward and pressed against a tree.

In a primal way, the woman bit through the cord, severing it from her egg. Then, she took the egg and held it close, cradling it.

"Demon…" Lord Jameson murmured from through his

surprise. Then, he shouted, "Ye be a *demon*!"

He took a heavy stone from the ground and hurried toward the woman. When he reached her, he hit it hard against her forehead, knocking her unconscious. Then, he continued to beat her head with the stone until he was certain she was dead.

When he was done with her, he lifted the stone over the egg, but it had cracked when the woman dropped it. Now, tiny hands and feet were pushing out of the cracks. To him, they looked as human as the hands and feet of any baby he'd seen.

Lowering the bloody stone, he dropped it to the ground and reached for the egg, folding back chunks of it to see the child's face. The most beautiful emerald green eyes stared back at him. Nervously, he took the baby from the shell, saw it was a girl, and patted her tiny back. She began to breathe and cry.

In the house, he cleaned her and checked her for any marking that would show she was a demon. She was perfect, without even a birthmark or freckle.

Lord Jameson could not bear to kill his daughter. She favored him remarkably so, even if she had hatched from an egg. He also could not return to the village or his family home with her. Questions would be asked about the mother, and in her current state, he would not be able to provide a body, lest it be known he had killed her.

Thusly, he chose to stay in the house of snakes and raised the little girl away from all other humans. He named her Adalinda, meaning noble serpent.

Adalinda grew up as most girls, playing in the flower patches and loving all things beautiful. Her father was quite proud of the child he'd raised, and despite knowing what she truly was, he loved her.

Lord Jameson died suddenly one afternoon when Adalinda was fourteen. While hunting in the forest, he was attacked by a troll and eaten. Adalinda had been playing nearby when it happened. She heard his screams, and when she reached him, the troll was feasting on his guts.

Frantic, she returned to the house and barricaded herself inside, on the off chance that the troll had seen her and followed. She waited inside in fear for three days, but the troll never showed up. She decided then to hunt the troll down and claim vengeance for her fallen father. When she found the beastly creature on the far side of the forest, she killed him mercilessly with her father's axe.

Bloody from the slaying, she dropped the axe where she stood and looked down at the nearly unrecognizable creature. She'd never killed anything before; her father had always handled the hunting for food. Adalinda wiped away a drizzle of blood that was crawling down her cheek. Then, she trembled.

In a fret, she rushed away from the fallen troll, leaving the axe behind. Tears began to fall from her eyes, and she wiped them away as she clumsily ran. Suddenly, she tripped and, unable to steady herself, she began to tumble down a steep hill. Twice, her head nearly knocked into the thick trunks of trees but she had been lucky and barely missed them.

Her tumbling roll slowed as she reached the foot of the hill and a clearing of trees. Scraped and scratched but otherwise unscathed, Adalinda stood and dusted herself off. Then, she stared through the clearing at the village just beyond a small meadow.

The meadow was filled with beautiful flowers in an array of colors, and the sight of it brightened her spirits. The sight of the village beyond it made her curious. Cautiously, she left the forest behind her and stepped to the meadow. She was nervous to do this, as she had never before left the safety of the forest or her beloved house. Her father had mentioned a village to her in the past, but when she'd asked why they couldn't visit, he had told her it was a place forbidden to them.

She never understood why, and now her father was dead. She thought of his mention of the village being forbidden, but instead of frightening her away from it, it only strengthened her curiosity. With her shoulders back and her head held high, she walked through the flowery meadow to the foot of the strange and intriguing village.

The village was bustling with activity and was filled with other people who didn't look all that dissimilar from Adalinda or her father. She smiled at this, as she'd often felt somewhat alone in the world.

There were more buildings than she could count, and as

some children ran by squealing with joy as they played, Adalinda felt herself growing overwhelmed with joy as well. She giggled at the children and then twirled on her heels to take in the whole sight. It was the most marvelous place she'd ever seen.

One of the children looked in her direction. The boy's eyes grew wide and his face stretched as he screamed. Then, faster than he'd been running before, he hurried far away from her.

She wondered what had frightened him so. Then, looking down at her hands and dress, she saw the troll's blood all over her. She, too, was bleeding from the slight wounds caused by her fall down the hill.

From her far right, she heard somebody gasp. Looking in that direction, she watched as a plump woman in a blue dress and a white apron set a large basket on the ground and hurried toward her.

"Ye poor girl!" the woman exclaimed as she got closer. "Look at ya! What a mess ya be! Who would have done this to such a lovely girl?"

Adalinda wasn't sure how she should respond. She knew she was a bloody mess, but she didn't want to tell the woman about the troll she'd just slaughtered. She was ashamed for having taken a life, even if it was the life of a vile creature that had deserved it.

"I... I fell," she told the plump, concerned woman. "I tripped and rolled down that hill." Turning toward the meadow, she pointed to the hilly forest beyond it.

"Oh, ye poor dear," the woman continued and took Adalinda by the elbow. "Come with me. Let us get ye cleaned up."

The woman led her to one of the quaint houses, and inside, she cleaned Adalinda's wounds. She also rummaged through some clothing and found a dress that looked like it may fit her.

"Try this on," she said and handed her the garment. "It belonged to me daughter. She won't be needing it any longer." The woman sighed but kept her smile. Her voice sounded sad to Adalinda, even though the smile was steady and pleasant.

"Do ye think yer daughter will mind?" Adalinda asked as she took the garment in her freshly cleansed hands. Its fabric was exquisitely soft – the softest of any she'd ever felt before.

"Nay," said the woman. "She left long ago, never to return…" Her voice trailed off at the end. Her gaze seemed lost as it drifted to the floor. "I hope ye like the dress. It be made of the finest silks known to man."

Indeed, Adalinda adored the garment. The feel and style of it were beyond anything she'd ever known. Gratefully, she dressed in it and admired her reflection in the looking glass. Unable to remain modest, she smiled giddily. This was the first time she had ever seen her reflection in anything other than fresh water at the creek. She thought she looked beautiful.

"Such a lovely lass ye be," the plump old woman told her. "Ah… yer nearly the spitting image of me daughter."

"Tell me what yer daughter was like," Adalinda asked,

turning around to face her host.

The kindly old woman beamed a little as her smile broadened. "She was the sweetest of anyone in the village," the woman explained in a warm and grandmotherly tone. "Beautiful, lively, and friendly, she was me pride and joy." She paused and wiped a tear from her eye. Adalinda offered her a comforting smile. After a moment, she continued. "She wanted so much to meet a nice lad and fall in love. She thought she met one too. One day while off on a walk in the forest, she happened upon a small house and the man of her precious dreams. When she came home to tell me about it, she claimed it to be love at first sight. Isn't that something, lassie? True love at first sight... Well, she had her mind made up right then and there, and she packed a bag, gave me a kiss on the cheek, and took off to live with her new love. After that... well, I never laid eyes on her again."

Adalinda's smile turned to a slight frown as she listened to the story of true love and then mysterious disappearance. She found it intriguing that this daughter had discovered her love in the very forest that she resided in. It gave her hope for a true love of her own, but at the same time, the daughter's disappearance made her leery.

"Perhaps she shall return to ye one day," she offered, believing it to be a possibility. "Perhaps she'll walk right through that door and ye shall be together again."

The woman smiled at her but shook her head. "Nay. Too

much time has passed. A mother knows when she has lost a child, and I know I have lost mine."

From somewhere nearby, Adalinda heard a hissing sound. Looking to the floor, she believed it to be coming from the old woman's basket. Curiously, she went to it and bent to lift the lid.

"I wouldn't do that, dearie," the plump grandmotherly host informed her. "That be one of the most deadly creatures on earth, given to me by a man on a voyage from a land far from here."

Adalinda pulled up from the basket and asked, "If it be so deadly, why dost ye have it?"

"Because to me," she answered, "it shows nothing but warmth and love."

Now more curious than before, Adalinda decided to chance her luck and bent to the basket once more. Carefully, she lifted its lid away. From within the basket, the most beautiful and majestic snake she'd ever seen rose up and slowly swayed from side to side, flickering its forked tongue at her.

"Be cautious," said the old woman. "No sudden movements."

Adalinda kept her eyes fixed with the snake's and smiled at it.

"The man called him King Cobra," the woman added. "He be one of the most venomous creatures in all of the known world."

"Hello, yer majesty," Adalinda told the snake. It flickered its tongue in reply and straightened. "I am Adalinda."

The snake rose up higher from his basket. The old woman took a cautious step toward them. Adalinda extended her elbow out and her forearm to the cobra.

"Ye shouldn't do that," the woman warned as the snake bobbed his head a bit.

Adalinda did not answer. Instead, she remained calm and patient, and after a short moment, the snake crawled up her arm and draped itself around her shoulders. His head rose beside Adalinda's, and as she stood upright, the two faced the old woman together.

"He seems quite friendly indeed," she told her host. The old woman's jaw fell slack. Her hands trembled at her sides. Adalinda watched the color drain from her rosy cheeks. "Is something the matter?" the girl asked.

Seemingly confused, the woman approached her and extended a hand to touch her cheek. Looking into her stunning green eyes, she smiled. It was then that Adalinda noticed her host had vibrant emerald green eyes also.

"Tell me, child... where is it ye say ye come from again?" She withdrew her shaky hand and awaited a response.

"Deep in the forest," she told her. "My father called our home the House of Snakes, due to the wood-carved snakes inside and out."

The old woman's grin stretched across her plump and wrinkled face. She looked down to one of the cuts on Adalinda's arm. "A fresh cut."

"From my tumble down the hill," Adalinda explained.

The old woman reached for the cut and grabbed hold of the slit skin. Adalinda flinched as she began to pull it, worsening the wound. Then, the young girl's eyes grew wide and amazed. The more the old woman pulled on her skin, the more she revealed what was beneath it – scales of green and black. Her host continued to pull away the skin until it was fully shed from Adalinda's forearm and hand.

"Yer like me," the plump old woman insisted, tearful once again. "Ye be me kin, child."

Adalinda listened to the woman's words as she stared in shock at her newly revealed scales. While her hand and arm were stunningly beautiful, she was confused and more than a bit frightened.

"Do not fear, lassie," the woman told her and took a few steps away. Adalinda looked at her and watched as her host began to peel her own skin away, shedding it and her clothing to the ground. When she was done, she was a plump serpent with two arms and two legs. The coloring of her scales was identical to that of Adalinda's.

Even though she was still confused, she quickly realized that she had somehow made her way to family she hadn't even known existed. As she stared into the serpent woman's eyes, she could see they were the same as hers. Slowly, she removed the silk dress and let it slip to the floor. Then, she slowly began to peel her human skin away, letting it flake and drop to the floor. After a moment, her skin was shed and she stood in a serpent form that she'd never known she had.

"Do not worry, dearie," the serpent woman told her and put her hand against Adalinda's scaly cheek. The touch was cooler than it had been before. "The skin will grow back in a few days. It will always grow back, I assure ye."

Having found family once more, along with finding her true self, Adalinda remained in the village and at the humble and quaint home of her elder kin. There, the two lived together happily ever after.

Congratulations, dearie! Thou hast navigated through twelve tales in the Book of Very Bad Things. *Perhaps ye can stomach one more? A baker's dozen, as they say.*

This final tale is perhaps the most scrumptious of all! It is about a jolly and very talented baker and his popular shoppe in a village. A master at creating unusual and tasty treats, the baker discovers great success, but like all success, it comes at a cost.

Dear reader... is that a patty cake yer about to eat? Ye might think twice after enjoying this deliciously sinister story. Here is our final mouthwatering tale, The Baker's Dozen.

The Baker's Dozen

There once was a kindly baker who provided the most delicious breads and pastries in his popular village shoppe. From before daybreak until well after nightfall, the baker busily tried out new ingredients, kneaded various wonderful breads, and created fillings and frostings that made the mouths water of anyone who tasted them.

Because of his special skills with tasty treats, the baker was incredibly popular within the village, and people made an effort to visit with him every chance they could.

On this particular day, the baker prepared scrumptious strawberry patty cakes. He topped them with fresh cream sweetened with strawberry juice. The strawberries were the ripest in the land and grown at the farm of his dear elder brother, who provided most of the dairy, grains and fruits that the baker required.

From the moment he opened his shoppe door and the morning sun lit his smiling mustached face, the baker knew it was going to be a busy day. Almost instantly, Missus Pennant and her small son Bipple wandered in. Missus Pennant insisted she needed only a loaf of grain bread, but the moment she and her son smelled the scent of the fresh strawberry patty cakes, they had to each have one. This was the pattern with nearly every customer who entered until he closed his door at noon. He'd sold out of patty cakes much more quickly than he'd thought, and it was time to make another batch.

"Ho, ho!" he chuckled as he stirred the ingredients in a large wooden bowl. "Twelve for them. One for me. A baker's dozen works out *perfectly*!" Sure enough, his fresh batch of strawberry batter prepared thirty-nine more strawberry patty cakes – three baker's dozen.

He ate his three quickly, licking his fingers and smacking his lips joyously after the last bite. Then, he opened his shoppe door once more and continued to serve the eager and hungry villagers. Word had quickly spread of the strawberry patty cakes, and the demand for them was again much greater than he'd prepared.

When he ran out, he repeated his earlier actions by closing his door and making twenty-six more patty cakes, equaling out to two baker's dozen. As before, the baker merrily feasted on his two patty cakes before opening the door to sell and serve the rest.

"This is wonderful!" exclaimed Mister Wayforne, who was the men's tailor for the village. "I must have one to take to my wife."

"She gets the last one," the baker told him giddily as he prepared the treat for the order. "I hope yer wife enjoys it."

"Oh, she will!" Mister Wayforne insisted. "At least, she will if this delicious patty cake even makes it home. I may just very well eat it myself!"

The baker chuckled at the man as he paid and left with the treat. The moment Mister Wayforne was gone, he closed up his shoppe for the day.

Having run out of fresh strawberries and a few other supplies, and still having a few hours left in the daylight, he grabbed a decent sized basket and headed off toward his brother's farm. When he reached it, he discovered that the strawberries were gone, as were all of the fresh fruits. They'd been picked away by the birds. Their bushes and vines were bare.

Devastated, the baker began his walk home. By the time he reached the village, it was nighttime and all was quiet. He glanced at his closed shoppe as he walked in the direction of his house. With a sigh, he pouted pitifully.

In the morning when he opened, the villagers would expect him to have something delicious and fresh for them – something that they would love and enjoy as if it was the greatest treat in the world. Something that would cause their sweet tooths to guide them into ecstasy...

He had no clue what that something would be now. He'd counted on those strawberries, or even the blackberries from the bushes, but they were gone. Birds had stolen his ingredients and feasted away his earnings for tomorrow.

From somewhere nearby, he heard someone whimper. There were few porch lanterns lit, and so everything was dark and shadowed. He stopped walking and listened more intently. The whimper seemed more like a cry, and it was coming from near the wishing well at the fountain.

Hurriedly, he went to it and sought the source of the cry. On the ground, he found a young peasant girl holding her calve and crying in pain.

"M'lady, what has happened?" he asked her as he knelt down beside her.

She looked at him through teary eyes. "I – I stumbled and cut my leg pretty deep," she told him, sobbing with nearly every word. "It's bleeding, and I cannot walk on it."

The baker smiled at her. "Worry not, lassie. I shall take ye to my bakery and bandage ye up right."

He lifted her into his arms and carried her up the road to the bakery. Once they were inside, he sat her on a stool and grabbed some cloths from the back. With one of the cloths, he cleaned the blood from the wound. The other, he tied around her leg, putting pressure on the cut and stopping the bleeding.

"Oh, Mister Baker, I do not know how to thank thee," she said to him as he stepped away to throw the bloody rag into a pile with other dirty rags. "I cannot imagine anyone else showing me such kindness."

He noticed he'd gotten some of her blood on his fingers as he'd cleaned the wound. He stared at his fingers for a moment and then rubbed the blood between them. Coyly, he sniffed them. The blood had a unique scent to it – one that he'd never really thought of before. Curiously, he licked a bit from a finger and tasted it. It was surprisingly sweet and delicious.

"I do not know what I would have done had ye not come around," the young woman continued from the front room. "Everything felt so dire! Ye be a saving grace for certain!"

"Think nothing of it," he said slowly and almost too lowly for her to hear as he looked at the remaining blood on his fingers. Swiftly, he licked the rest away. "Ye may need to have that sewn up."

"It will be fine," she replied as he stepped back into the room. "I have come to accept some things." She smiled. Her words were curious, but he thought she was lovely, even if she did have a few additional cuts and scabs on her face and hands. Her blood was immaculate though… delicious.

"Nourishment first," he told her and took a piece of pound cake from his counter top and handed it to her. "Eat this. Ye must be hungry."

"How gracious!" the peasant exclaimed and accepted the pound cake. A moan slipped from her lips as she ate it.

Also from the counter, the baker took his bread knife. While the woman was distracted with her treat, he came around behind her and pulled her hair back. The knife sliced through her neck before she had a chance to make a sound. When she did try to scream, it was low and gargled.

He took a step back and watched her fall from the chair to the floor. He watched as the blood spilled from her neck and realized he was wasting it. He took a bowl and placed it beneath her neck, letting the blood pour into it. When it was full, he filled a second bowl.

Two bowls of this new sweet syrup were enough, he thought as he pulled the woman's body into the backroom and began to cut it up. She had much blood left and it spilled out onto the floor as she was chopped to pieces. He let that blood go to waste, knowing he'd never be able to use that much tomorrow and fearing that any left over would surely spoil. Once she was in small enough pieces, he put them in a hefty bag and carried her out into the forest. There, he scattered her around for the wild animals to eat and enjoy.

Back in his beloved shoppe, the baker cleaned up the mess of the spilled blood and then prepared his ingredients for the morning. When everything was ready and shipshape for tomorrow, he closed up again and headed home.

The baker was a single man and lived in a small three-room cottage just a few minutes' walk from his shoppe. Once home, he prepared a small snack at his little wooden table and then changed for bed. In bed, he was giddy over the prospects of tomorrow. He knew this new sweetener would be an even greater sensation than the strawberry patty cakes had been. The villagers would love his new creation, and if it was as successful as the baker hoped, he knew his special ingredient was in no short supply.

He slept and his head filled with dreams of happy smiling faces, all eating delicious treats made by his own two talented hands. The dreams made him smile in his sleep, and he awoke at his usual time with the smile still there.

The baker hummed pleasantly as he dressed and readied for the new day. He sipped a spot of cold tea and snacked on stale biscotti he'd made a week ago. Then, grabbing his apron from beside the door, he headed off to work.

Utilizing the fresh and cool blood as a sweetener, he made a trial batch of two patty cakes. When they'd cooled enough, he tasted one. His body nearly numbed as a blissful feeling of nirvana overcame him. Never before had the baker ever tasted something so... delicately *perfect*. It was the most deliciously sweet cake he'd ever had. It made goosebumps pop up all over his skin. He tingled slightly from head to toe, and he could swear the ends of his mustache curled up a little.

As if he was starved, he devoured the rest of the patty cake and the second one as well. After the last bite, he licked the remains of the flavor from his plump fingers and moaned with satisfaction.

There was no way this new treat would not be a success, he decided as he prepared the pans. "Ho! Ho!" He exclaimed as he portioned the batter out. "Twelve for them! One for me! A baker's dozen works out *perfectly*!"

He made six batches of thirteen patty cakes and then used the remaining blood to create a sweet crimson frosting that he spread over top each. Then, he chose his six from the seventy-eight frosted patty cakes and began to eat.

When he was finished, the baker felt fatter and full, but ultimately satisfied. He then readied the patty cakes for sale and opened his door for the day.

His first customer was Mister Boyles, who had stopped by midday yesterday and tried one of his strawberry patty cakes, as well as taking two loaves of bread.

"I just had to come by today and try one of yer strawberry patty cakes again!" Mister Boyles exclaimed anxiously.

"Oh, but, Mister Boyles," the baker told him, "I am afraid I have no more of those."

Mister Boyles looked immediately deflated. "I hate to hear it," he replied sadly. "They were wonderful."

"Aye," said the baker, "but I've something even *more* delectable prepared for today." Proudly, he waved a frosted red patty cake before the man's eyes. "Something new that I have made for ye."

Mister Boyles licked his lips as he stared at the culinary masterpiece. His mouth was practically watering. Looking back at the baker, he asked, "What is it called?"

It occurred to the baker that he had not yet chosen a name for his latest sweet treat. On the spot, he decided its name. "A heart cake," he said, handing it over. "Ye shall love it."

From the very first bite, Mister Boyles experienced a sensation that left him stunned and speechless. He savored that bite for a long while, taking his time with it as he moaned and gasped at the flavor. Then, almost savagely, he devoured the rest.

"Two more to go, if ye please," he requested with a blissful smile on his face.

The heart patty cakes were a grand success. As with the strawberry patty cakes yesterday, word of these new treats spread quickly throughout the village. Soon, he was overwhelmed with business and the supply of cakes quickly diminished.

When the there were only two heart patty cakes remaining, he sold one and kept the other for himself. Closing earlier than usual, he ate the cake at a much better pace than he'd enjoyed the six earlier. Being the last one, he nibbled on it here and there, licked at the frosting, and made sure that not a single crumb of it was wasted. Even though he took his time with it, it seemed to be gone and finished before he knew it.

"That was the best thing I've ever made," said the baker as he moped about his shoppe, mourning the end of the heart patty cakes. He glanced out the window and watched the people go to and fro, some stopping and noticing his closed door before moving on. Then, he smiled. There were many people in this village, and so far, no one seemed to have missed the peasant girl. Why did today have to be the end of the heart patty cakes? Why couldn't he sell them tomorrow too? All he needed was more ingredients... well, one ingredient that he just happened to be out of.

He waited patiently in his shoppe for the time to pass and the sun to set. Coyly, he kept watch out the window, noting who was out and about and who was with other people. He had to be sneaky about this. He had to pick just the right one at just the right time.

The baker grew anxious and a bit more giddy as time continued to pass and the thick of the crowd dwindled into just a few strays. Rubbing his hands together, he said, "Patty cakes, oh, patty cakes! How people love thee!"

If he was able to produce for tomorrow something as scrumptiously wonderful as he'd presented today, his patty cakes would sell out faster than ever. He would make twice as many this time, he decided. Even if he didn't sell every one of them, the extras would not go to waste. He'd ensure that personally.

He realized that this latest endeavor had the potential to make him a very wealthy man as well. Once he made enough money off of these peasants, he could move to a better part of the kingdom, and perhaps he could work his way into the castle and become a personal baker for the King, himself.

Oh, how that dream sounded remarkable and wonderful to the baker. His eyes lit up as he envisioned it, and he was all ready to start packing up his belongings to move into the castle when he heard a knock at his shoppe door.

"Now, who could that be?" he muttered to himself as he looked at the door. Surely, whoever it was knew that he was closed, being as late as it was. Perhaps his light let them know he was there. With a huff, he went to the door and opened it. A small mousy-looking woman in a black dress and a red cloak stood on the other side. She had a large scab on her cheek, as if she'd been attacked by a wild dog. Her eyes were wide and pleading.

"Please, Mister Baker," she said in a weak and trembling tone. "Might I have a moment of yer time?"

The baker sighed and stepped back from the door to allow her entry. He didn't want to turn her away; she may have wanted to buy something. "But of course, madam," he replied.

The woman walked in with the use of a cane held by a trembling and badly wounded hand. She looked up at the baker; tears were filling her eyes. He shut the door behind her.

"I hate to bother ye," she told him. "I have asked everybody in town, but no one knows… No one has seen her."

"Seen who?" he inquired. He hoped she wasn't referencing whom he thought she was referencing.

"Me daughter," she whispered. The baker swallowed down a lump in his throat. "She ran off late last night in a panic, and she never came home."

He smiled and chuckled nervously. "A panic, ye say? Perhaps… perhaps she ran into the woods? There are wolves in those woods, ya know."

"Goblins, too," she said worriedly and softly nodded her head.

"What does she look like?" he questioned, eager to know for sure if this was the peasant girl from last night.

The woman described her daughter in great detail – everything from the clothes she wore to the color of her eyes and hair. It was, without a doubt, the girl he'd killed.

The baker sighed and folded his arms over his round belly, full of her daughter's delicious patty cakes. "Nay, madam," he told her in a sad way. "I sure wish I knew more to tell ya."

She nodded her head again and turned back to the door. The baker opened it for her. "Thank ye," she said as she stepped outside. Looking back at him, she beckoned, "Please, Mister Baker, if she happens by, please ask her to come home immediately. We shall be moving in the morning from this land."

He smiled and nodded at her assuringly. The fact that the family was moving made things a bit easier for him, even if he had to question why she would leave her daughter behind after being gone for only one day. "Aye, madam. I shall do that."

"Oh," she said and turned toward him once more. "Please, take great caution, Mister Baker, if ye do happen to see her."

"Great caution?" He huffed. "For what?"

"The leprosy, Mister Baker," she answered, and his heart nearly stopped. "It be incredibly contagious. We are being moved to the camp in the morning."

The woman walked off into the night and the baker felt himself grow flushed with immediate dread and horrifying terror. Dozens of the villagers had eaten the heart patty cakes. They'd all ingested the blood of a leper, and soon, they would start showing signs of the disease, as would anyone that they've been in close contact with.

He too would soon show signs of the horrible disease. He would not be moving into the castle and working for the King, nor would he become richer than his wildest dreams. He would, instead, watch as his body deteriorated and decayed even as he continued to live. He would be exiled to the leper camp, if he wasn't first executed for spreading it throughout the village.

Surely, no one would know it was he that spread the plague. Certainly, no one would ever guess the poisoned blood had been in his very own patty cakes. While this gave him hope for his reputation, it did nothing to help the evitable. The entire village would soon become plagued with leprosy, and it would be a devastating nightmare for everyone involved.

Doing the only thing he knew to do, he spent the night making three hundred and ninety special patty cakes – thirty baker's dozen. These, he gave away for free until every last one was gone. These patty cakes contained a special combination of herbs from the forest. First, sleep settled in an hour or so after it was ingested. Then, the heart stopped, providing a gentle death.

The next morning, the streets of the village were empty.

Not a soul was to be seen or heard. Nobody but the baker, who had saved his thirty patty cakes for last.

"Ho... ho..." he muttered as he brought the first one to his lips. "A dozen for them... one for me... A baker's dozen works out *perfectly*." Closing his eyes, he took the first bite. Then, forcing himself through the process, he ate all of the patty cakes that he could until he simply fell asleep and died.

See now, that wasn't so bad, was it, dearie? Don't tell me the Book of Very Bad Things *has frightened ye. Surely, ye shall sleep soundly and with pleasant dreams tonight. After those wonderful tales, I know I will!*

Yes... the hour is getting late. I suppose it is time for us to part ways now. I have a long day tomorrow of potions, spells, and havoc. I'm sure ye must have something important to do as well. Thusly, goodnight and thank ye, dear reader. It has been lovely spending this time with ye. I certainly hope we bump into one another again in the future. Until then, take care.

Oh, now... before I forget, I have a riddle for ye. If ye can answer it, ye shall sleep safe and sound. If ye cannot answer it, have no fear. The answer shall come to thee eventually.

It always comes, never too late. Sometimes, it's early. Sometimes, ye wait. Often presumed; often avoided. Rarely ever is it ever voided. In the night or in the day, whilst at work or whilst at play, it always knows when it's time to convey.

Good luck, dearie, and pleasant dreams!

And as they say in the storybooks, "The End!"

Madame Howell

DCL Publications, LLC

http://www.thedarkcastlelords.net

Find our books at any fine online retailer.